# "IT'S ARMED TO THE TEETH!"

Donovan noted the distance to the target on the screen. In a minute the chopper would be within weapons-mode range. "Cease probe," he ordered.

"Probe deactivated."

"Switch to weapons-mode."

"Switching."

Communications Officer Jennings suddenly twisted a dial on his monitor. "Captain, they've activated a laser rangefinder in their nose. They have us locked in their missile sights."

Donovan came out of his chair, his pulse pounding. The sons of bitches were going to fire!

# RAVEN RISING

## J.D. CAMERON

AVON BOOKS ◆ NEW YORK

OMEGA SUB #6: RAVEN RISING is an original publication of Avon Books. This work has never before appeared in book form. This work is a novel. Any similarity to actual persons or events is purely coincidental.

AVON BOOKS
A division of
The Hearst Corporation
1350 Avenue of the Americas
New York, New York 10019

First Avon Books Printing: May 1992

AVON TRADEMARK REG. U.S. PAT. OFF. AND IN OTHER COUNTRIES, MARCA REGISTRADA, HECHO EN U.S.A.

Printed in the U.S.A.

RA 10 9 8 7 6 5 4 3 2 1

# Prologue

Executive Officer John Percy of the U.S.S. *Liberator* stood on the narrow strip of shoreline bordering Saint Andrew Sound and anxiously scanned the dark surface of the water. Stars sparkled in the heavens and crickets chirped in the woods at his rear. A cool breeze from the northwest stirred his hair. He hefted the submachine gun in his right hand and wondered if any of the dreaded white-shirts were abroad this night.

Undoubtedly they were.

The zombies were everywhere.

Percy wasn't too worried about being discovered. He wore a skintight black bodysuit, enabling him to blend into the background. Slanted across his chest were two black utility belts crammed with spare magazines for his Franchi plus extra clips for the Colts snug in their holsters at his waist. In other pockets were rations, a compass, plenty of matches, rope, and additional items needed to survive in a world gone insane. As if the guns weren't enough of an arsenal, grenades were clipped to the edges of both chest belts. To cap off his possessions, a transceiver rode on his left hip behind the Colt.

How much longer? Percy wondered. Would the sub arrive tonight or the next? It should be there soon if all had gone well. A big if. Already it was a day late.

1

A loud splash came from the sound.

Startled, Percy swung in its direction and peered intently into the gloom, striving to identify the source. Common sense told him a fish had been responsible, but gone were the carefree days when a person could rely on rational judgment to explain everyday occurrences. World War Three had forever altered the nature of things.

He crouched, gripping the Franchi in both hands, the feel of the steel against his palms reassuring. The Navy version of the Luigi Franchi 9-mm automatic sported a 32-round box magazine and could fire 250 rounds per minute, a particularly lethal piece of hardware in the right hands. And Percy knew how to use his. The weapon had been a favorite of armed forces and guerilla groups for years, having replaced the once ubiquitous Uzi as the most dependable submachine gun on the market. Of course, that was back when there had *been* a market.

Chiding himself for having a bad case of nerves, Percy relaxed and straightened. Not that he felt guilty or foolish. Since *Liberator* had dropped them off they'd fought an unending battle against the vile white-shirts and contended with wildlife gone amok. But the effort had been worth it. They'd saved two children from a horrible fate and—

The transceiver suddenly crackled softly and a whispering voice spoke urgently.

"Red Three to Red Two. Red Three to Red Two."

Percy whipped the transceiver to his mouth and pressed the send button. "Red Two here. What is it?"

"Trouble, sir. We've got company. White-shirts."

"On my way, Burroughs," Percy said, whirling and racing to the northwest, heedless of the noise he made. He threaded among the trees, skirting thickets and vaulting logs, ignoring the branch tips and brush that tugged at his clothing or nicked his neck and face, keenly aware that the seaman wouldn't have broken radio silence unless it was an emergency, and determined to get there in time to help.

Gunfire crackled in the distance, from the direction of the farmhouse half a mile away.

The sound galvanized Percy to greater effort. He ran as he'd never run before. If he tripped or hit a tree or a boulder in the darkness he might be severely injured, but he didn't care. Reaching Burroughs and the Williams kids, Randy and Janet, was all that mattered. His heart pounded in his chest, his blood pounded in his temples, and his shoes pounded the earth.

As Percy ran, his mind raced back in time three nights to the daring rescue of the children in Argyle, Georgia. A band of desperate survivors had been overrun by a horde of savage white-shirts and the zombies were in the act of feeding the few defiant humans still alive to huge bonfires when he'd arrived in the town with Burroughs. Together they'd been able to free the children. And he'd be damned if he'd let anything happen to them now.

The shooting briefly let up, then resumed more fiercely.

Hang on! Percy wanted to shout. Instead, he devoted all of his energy to sprinting northwestward. So focused was he on the terrain ahead that he nearly missed spotting the white-garbed figure perhaps thirty feet off to his left.

One of the crazies!

The realization brought him to an abrupt stop, so abrupt he almost tripped over his own feet. He pivoted and saw the zombie shuffling toward the farmhouse, drawn by the shooting, just one of dozens or scores or hundreds of ghoulish reinforcements hastening to the scene at that very second. Goose bumps erupted all over his skin and he had to force his legs forward.

3

Percy kept his eyes on the emaciated figure and observed it twist violently his way when it spied him. Instantly the demented scarecrow altered course, giving chase. Thankfully, the majority of white-shirts were slow movers, physically unable to run at the full speed of a healthy human because of their frail, deteriorating bodies. And therein lay the paradox.

White-shirts were believed to be the result of the incredibly huge amounts of radiation spread across the country during the war. The radiation, according to *Liberator*'s chief medical specialist, had mutated a neurotropic virus. Those afflicted suffered an extreme neurological and mental disorder, their minds essentially gone, their bodies wasting away. Yet they were endowed with superhuman strength. In large packs they were virtually unstoppable.

How big was the pack attacking the farmhouse? Percy reflected as he came to the edge of the woods. Beyond lay a meadow, and at the opposite end reared the abandoned building. Burroughs was on the second floor, firing from a window, tiny spurts of reddish orange flame flashing from the Franchi's muzzle with each burst.

Zombies were converging from all directions.

Percy gasped at the sight of dozens crossing the meadow. They were strung out in loose order. None were in his immediate vicinity. If he waited to make his move, more would arrive, and the greater their numbers the less his chances of reaching his companions. He had no choice.

His stomach muscles involuntarily tightening, Percy worked the cocking handle on his Franchi, took a deep breath, and sprinted forward.

A grenade went off in the yard near the house, briefly illuminating the tableau, showing twenty or thirty ghouls already there, most congregated at the back door.

Percy knew the fiends were trying to batter their

4

way inside. He gritted his teeth and ran past several white-shirts, inhaling their putrid odor and suppressing an urge to gag.

One of the zombies vented a hideous shriek.

Others turned at the sound and discovered the human in their midst. A chorus of bellows, hisses, and inarticulate cries rent the air.

Now I'm in for it, Percy grimly thought, and let the surging adrenaline in his system fuel his limbs. Less than two hundred yards separated him from the farmhouse, two hundred yards and half that many sore-covered monstrosities eager to tear him apart.

A thin man wearing a grime-covered white smock closed in from the right. In his right hand he clutched a crowbar.

On the left were a pair of fleet zombies armed with crude clubs, broken sections of tree limbs.

Percy never slowed. He levelled the Franchi and stroked the trigger, gratified at the blasting of the weapon and the dark dots that blossomed on Crowbar's chest. The man was hurled onto his back, twitching convulsively.

Not missing a beat, Percy whipped the Franchi in an arc and fired again, the rounds drilling the other pair and felling them flat.

The enraged chorus became louder.

Percy continued grimly onward, alertly glancing right and left, wary of being taken unawares. His shots had attracted those zombies still ignorant of his arrival and now most of those in the meadow were focusing on him instead of the farmhouse. Good. He'd taken some of the heat off Burroughs.

Another grenade lit up the backyard, revealing over a dozen corpses littering the ground.

Another white-shirt drew too close for comfort, and Percy perforated the sickly figure with well-placed slugs. As he ran he mentally worked out the logistics of their escape. Somehow he had to get Burroughs and the kids from the farmhouse into the barn, where their wheels were stashed. Once in the souped-up Chevelle he could leave the zombies in the dust.

A shout came from the house, Burroughs bellowing out, "Hurry, sir! I can't hold them off much longer!"

Accenting the point there arose a muted scream from within the home.

That must be Janet! Percy realized, and tried to go faster, shifting his gaze between the crazies and the house, between the crazies and the house, never once looking down because he assumed the level meadow posed no obstacles to his passage. He was wrong.

The very next moment his right foot hit a hole and he crashed onto his elbows, wrenching his leg in the bargain. Quickly he sat up and tried to push to his feet, but his ankle was wedged in the hole and wouldn't budge.

All around him the white-shirts swarmed ever closer.

Frantically Percy placed his left palm on the ground and shoved, to no avail. He guessed that he'd blundered into a groundhog burrow but had no time or inclination to confirm the deduction.

Shrieking maniacally, a zombie wielding an axe swooped toward the officer.

Percy snapped off a burst, seeing the man's head snap back and the guy drop. He twisted, grimacing at the pain in his leg, and saw more coming from his rear. If he didn't get out of there, he was dead.

A third grenade boomed near the house.

Bracing both hands now, Percy pushed and pushed, sweat beading his brow, the veins on his neck standing out as he struggled.

A viperish hissing announced one of his unnatural adversaries.

Percy turned to the right and there was a woman holding a makeshift spear poised for a thrust. He attempted to bring the Franchi up but he was too late.

The woman cackled and swept the spear point at his chest.

Throwing himself backwards Percy evaded the strike, although the tip gouged into his blacksuit, tearing the fabric. His left hand swooped to the corresponding Colt and streaked the pistol free.

Sputtering, her mouth flecked with foam, the woman raised the spear for a second try.

Percy pointed the Colt at her forehead and at almost point-blank range cored her brain, the single crack bucking his arm upward, the woman catapulting rearward and landing in a miserable crumpled heap.

Undeterred, the remaining zombies were eagerly advancing.

There were too many to fight while trapped, Percy realized, and gulped. Holstering the Colt, he applied all of his strength to escaping from the hole. His leg was wedged to several inches above the ankle, and the hard earth dug into his sock and skin. He ignored the torment and shoved, shoved, shoved.

As if sensing he couldn't get away, the white-shirts had slowed and were forming a ring around him, a wall of putrid flesh and blank eyes, of clawed fingers and teeth exposed in mindless, feral rage.

Percy gave up trying to extricate his leg. He grabbed the Franchi, removed the partially spent magazine, and slapped home a fresh one. Under no circumstances would he permit the creatures to take him alive. Being burnt to a crisp was *not* an appealing demise. His right hand closed on a grenade.

The white-shirts were shoulder to shoulder and slowly closing the net.

This is it, Percy thought, and jerked the pineapple from the belt. He inserted a finger into the pull ring

7

and tensed his arm. The crazies were so close that he might be caught in the kill radius but he had no choice.

Those on the left were only twenty-five feet from him.

Inhaling, Percy yanked the ring, tossed the grenade, and hugged the ground. He draped both arms protectively over his head and ears, closing his eyes as he mouthed a silent prayer for deliverance.

The detonation was deafening, a thunderous roar that shook the earth and flared bright light for a score of yards. Dirt granules, clods of earth, bits of vegetation and pieces of ruptured bodies rained down.

Percy winced as a heavy object struck him between the shoulder blades and fell to one side. He lifted his head, coughing in the cloud of dust and smoke swirling about him, and saw a severed arm lying nearby.

The white-shirts were temporarily obscured by the cloud.

Grabbing another grenade, Percy waited impatiently for the dust and other particles to disperse, hoping against hope that the blast had checked the zombies' advance. He held his breath, his eyes narrowed, striving to pierce the gradually dissipating veil. At last he did.

Instead of halting, the white-shirts were now closer than before and already filling the gap caused by the explosion. Quite a few had been injured, losing an arm, a leg, or suffering a torn torso, yet still they came on, hideous, unstoppable nightmares grotesquely lumbering forward for the kill.

The outcome was inevitable. Percy let go of the second grenade. Using it now would be certain suicide and he'd rather take more of them with him. He pressed the Franchi to his right shoulder, touched his finger to the trigger, and prepared to sell his life as dearly as possible.

8

At that moment, over six hundred miles to the north, Captain Thomas P. Donovan sat in the bow of an inflatable, a Franchi tucked between his bent knees, and fumed with annoyance. "A day wasted," he muttered. "I should have known better."

One of the three blacksuit-clad crewmen who were paddling the inflatable down the murky waterway known as the James River heard the remark and looked at his commanding officer. "What choice did you have, sir? You couldn't ignore a distress call."

"No, I couldn't," Donovan begrudgingly admitted, although the justification did little to soothe his irritation. He thought of Percy and Burroughs, no doubt anxiously awaiting the sub's arrival at the rendezvous point, and frowned.

Had it only been slightly over twenty-four hours ago that *Liberator* was en route from her successful rescue mission to the devastated Big Apple when Communications Officer Jennings received a faint Mayday on the shortwave band? It seemed longer, probably because it had taken forever to negotiate the Hampton Roads channel due to the sunken vessels obstructing passage.

Norfolk, Virginia, the metropolis on the south side of the channel, had sustained a direct hit, an air burst that must have reduced the population from over 300,000 to 30,000 in the blink of an eye.

Donovan had not been surprised to find Norfolk in ruins; as one of America's top shipping ports and the site of the nation's largest naval installation, the Norfolk Naval Base, the city had been rated as a primary target.

But the amount of wreckage and other debris cluttering Hampton Roads had been somewhat unexpected. He'd sat in his command chair for over twelve hours watching young Helmsman Hooper carefully pick a safe path inland. Once past Norfolk there had still been problems with oceangoing vessels either partly submerged or littering the bottom. Because the James River was a tidal waterway, the largest of ships had been able to travel in from the Atlantic Ocean some sixty-six miles to Hopewell.

Finally arriving there, Donovan had gone ashore with the three seamen and traveled almost due west to the town of Chester, where the distress call originated. And what had they found? He scowled, remembering the sophisticated ham setup operating on battery power and automatically broadcasting the Mayday every ten minutes as the owner undoubtedly programmed it to do. There had been no sign of the operator, although dried pools of blood outside the radio shack had indicated his or her likely fate.

Chalk the life of another survivor up to the damn white-shirts, Donovan reflected, and shook his head to dispel his morbid introspection. He took a breath of the humid air, listening to the paddles lap at the water.

"I'll be glad to get back on the ship, sir," the same seaman commented eagerly.

"You and me both," Donovan agreed, shifting to peer to the southeast. *Liberator* should be close, her profile appearing at any second.

"I'm also happy we didn't bump into too many white-shirts," the man added.

Donovan simply nodded. They had seen several roving bands of the primarily nocturnal predators, but none of the zombies had spotted them. He hoped Percy and Burroughs had also been as fortunate.

On the north side of the river there suddenly arose a piercing, protracted howl.

"A dog, you think, Captain?" another of the crewmen wondered.

"Must be," Donovan said. There certainly weren't any wolves in Virginia unless one had escaped from a zoo, and there weren't any coyotes as far as he knew. Then again, who was he to say? Mother Nature had gone amok after the holocaust, the wildlife being afflicted by the same radiation psychosis that bred the white-shirts. Animals everywhere now attacked humans with no provocation. Dogs, cats, and even certain birds were implacable enemies of the same humans who once fed and cared for them. Dog packs were quite common.

A second howler chimed in as the first cry tapered off, followed by other canine voices forming into a strangely haunting primitive choir.

"That gives me the creeps," remarked the tallest seaman.

Donovan found the howling oddly comforting. Simply knowing other forms of life still existed, hostile or not, reassured him that the task he'd set for *Liberator* and her crew, namely striving to rebuild the world from scratch, wasn't a hopeless case. Ever since relocating dozens of survivors from San Francisco to the South Pacific island of Espiritu, where they were busily getting on with their lives in a paradise free from contamination, he'd been increasingly optimistic about starting over. He was realistic enough to know it would take time, lots and lots of time. Rome, so the old saying went, hadn't been built in a day. Nor would the world be.

"Look there, sir," a crewman said, pointing to the northeast.

11

Several raging bonfires, perhaps five hundred yards from the shoreline, revealed the presence of zombies. Stick figures moved about in front of the flames, involved in their senseless crusade of burning anyone and everyone who wasn't a white-shirt—whether alive or dead.

"I pray they don't have any survivors," said one of the sailors.

Donovan stared at the flickering fires and shuddered. While the howling had given him hope, the white-shirts tended to confirm that humankind's consummate insanity might well culminate in the utter elimination of the human race from the face of the planet. Not that the planet would miss the lowly fleas much. After centuries of having her seas, rivers, and land polluted beyond reclamation and her myriad creatures driven to the brink of extinction, maybe the Earth wanted to be cleansed of the vermin infesting her biosphere.

"There's the ship, Captain!"

Donovan looked and beamed. There could be no mistaking the outline of the 400-foot nuclear powered Omega-class submarine at anchor thirty yards away. *Liberator*, he proudly recalled, had been the most advanced sub in the U.S. fleet at the outbreak of the conflict. Crammed with technological marvels that would make any scientist or engineer drool, she was designed to serve the twofold purpose of warship and seaborne colony.

The huge vessel looming ever nearer belied a little-known fact concerning her crew complement, personnel Donovan regarded as the best ever to man a ship. Because of the extent to which *Liberator* was automated, shipboard systems once requiring several men to operate now required only one. Instead of having a crew of 120, typical of comparably sized nuclear subs, *Liberator* managed quite nicely with a crew of 45. Her spacious compartments, duty stations, and recreational facilities were almost luxurious. Everyone had their own cabin, the officers their own heads and showers.

"Let's see if anyone is home," Donovan joked, unclipping his transceiver from his belt. "Red One to *Liberator*. Do you copy?"

"Five by, Captain," came the immediate response in the calm voice of Communications Officer Dave Jennings. "Are you okay?"

"Fine. Get a detail topside to meet us. We'll be there before you know it."

"Any luck, sir?" Jennings asked hopefully.

"I wish. Another dud, I'm afraid. Have you picked up anything new while we were gone?"

"Negative, Captain. The airwaves are as dead as a graveyard."

An appropriate comparison, Donovan wryly mused. "All right. Get that detail up on deck and inform Flazy that we'll be under way as soon as I'm back on the bridge."

"Aye, sir,"

"Donovan out." He clicked off and watched as *Liberator*'s running lights came on and a half-dozen men scrambled out of the forward hatch onto the foredeck. They quickly moved to the port diving plane, several smiling and waving in greeting.

Returning the courtesy, Donovan gazed at the bonfires. He wasn't worried about the white-shirts spotting the ship's lights. From prior encounters with the zombies he knew they were unable to swim. Lacking the necessary arm and leg coordination to so much as dog paddle, any crazies who entered deep water invariably drowned.

The paddles were raised as the inflatable glided the remaining few feet and a line was tossed to the waiting seamen on the sub, who in moments had the little craft secured and were offering its occupants congratulations on getting back in one piece.

"We tried real hard," Donovan quipped, handing over his Franchi. He hastened to the hatch and

13

quickly went down the ladder. When he reached the bridge all hands looked up.

"Welcome back, Captain," Communications Officer Jennings declared from his duty station.

"Did you miss me?" Donovan asked absently, striding to his comfortable swivel chair situated immediately to the rear of the helmsman's post.

"No."

General mirth ensued.

Donovan chuckled and stared at the wondrous Cyclops display, noting the position of the anchored sub in relation to the north and south shores and the depth under the keel.

Cyclops derived its name from its official title, Cycle Optics, the typically bureaucratic designation for an extraordinary system that projected three-dimensional holographic images with startling clarity and depth of perception. The system took information from *Liberator*'s sensors, including primarily sonar but also radar, UHF, and satellite feeds when available, and integrated all the info into a shimmery blue-and-green light display that seemed to hover in the air in front of and partly surrounding the helmsman's and captain's posts. All subsea terrain, surface conditions, and the sea itself (or whatever other waterway the sub was in) were accurately depicted with astonishing realism.

For all its remarkable capability, Cyclops was but one of many unique aspects of the ship. Another innovative technological breakthrough incorporated a pair of laser turrets into an effective data-gathering and tactical weapons system. An outgrowth of laser research originally devoted to surface-to-sub communications, the lasers could be employed at ranges up to 10,000 yards to gather information or at a reduced range of up to 1,000 yards as a weapon able to severely disrupt electrical circuits. When tied into Cyclops, they could also provide pinpoint accuracy on any target. The turrets were located fore and aft of the tower.

"As soon as everyone is below, get set to bring the ship about, Mr. Hooper," Donovan said.

"Gladly, sir," the helmsman replied. Only nineteen, Dave Hooper was the youngest member of the crew but knew more about *Liberator*'s design specifications and inner workings than anyone else on board with the possible exception of Chief Engineer Smith, who years ago had acquired the unfortunate nickname Flazy due to his exaggerated reputation for being fat and lazy. The pair were often seen in the mess arguing various points about the sub in an effort to prove who was more knowledgeable.

Donovan placed his right elbow on the arm of his chair and rested his chin in his palm. No sooner had he done so than a soft, feminine voice whispered in his ear.

"They might not have missed you, lover, but I certainly did."

Straightening, Donovan gazed fondly into the eyes of the woman who, miracle of miracles, cared for him with all her heart. "Hi, Alex," he said.

Alexandra Fisher's lovely features became mildly reproachful. The daughter of an Episcopalian minister, she had luxurious dark hair that fell past her slim shoulders; high, prominent cheekbones; and a narrow face that conveyed just a hint of her forceful, resourceful personality. She wore a blue jumpsuit that adequately covered her shapely figure. As the only woman on *Liberator*, she felt it wise not to accent her inherent sensuality. "Is that all you can say after being gone for twenty-four hours? Hi, Alex?"

"I can hardly sweep you into my arms in front of the men, now, can I?" Donovan rejoined, grinning.

Alex leaned forward so only he would hear. "I suppose not. I'll take a rain check and you can ravish me later."

"Have you no shame, wench?"

"No. And if you call me a wench again, I'll rip your face off."

Donovan laughed and affectionately caressed her chin. His eyes strayed to her abdomen and he whispered, "Besides, is it safe to ravish you in your condition?"

"I won't break," Alex said, her eyes twinkling. "And bear in mind that just because I'm late doesn't necessarily mean I'm in the family way."

"A guy can always hope."

"Do you mean that?"

"Yes," Donovan said sincerely, and noticed Hooper looking back at them. "We'll talk about this later." He cleared his throat. "Yes, Mr. Hooper?"

"The men have the inflatable below, sir, and the hatch has been sealed."

"Then raise anchor and move into the outbound shipping channel, if you please."

"Yes, sir."

Both shipping channels in the James River had been redredged by the Army Corps of Engineers several years before the war and there existed plenty of room for *Liberator* to maneuver. Hooper handled her superbly, as if sub and man were an extension of one another.

"What have you been doing while I was gone?" Donovan asked Alex.

Before she could answer him an excited cry from Communications Officer Jennings electrified everyone on the bridge.

"Captain, multiple airborne contacts fifteen miles off and closing fast."

At the very instant Percy was about to fire an odd sound wafted down from the heavens, a faint whirring noise, a *thwip-thwip-thwip* repeated over and over and over. A powerful wind suddenly buffeted the zombies and swayed the high grasses and weeds.

Astounded, Percy gazed skyward and saw nothing at first. Then he distinguished the massive outline of . . . something . . . hovering a hundred or so feet up and forty feet to the west, blocking out the stars.

The white-shirts never bothered to glance up. In their virtually brain-dead state they were unable to realize the significance of the wind and the soft sound. The same mental impairment prevented them from displaying shock when, a second later, the sky rained death.

Percy heard a low metallic chatter and saw the crazies to his left start jerking convulsively as their bodies were perforated repeatedly by high-powered rounds. He flattened, afraid the aerial gunners might hit him by mistake.

In a devastating display of uncanny marksmanship, whoever was up there stitched a line of fire in a perfect circle, blistering the zombies, dropping them in droves where they stood. A few screamed in protest. Most went into eternity quietly, their dull

17

expressions no different after death than before.

Swiveling his head, Percy followed the hail of slugs all the way around. The whole incident took less than five seconds. Yet when the firing stopped there wasn't a white-shirt upright.

Elated, he stared at the mysterious black shape, striving to identify it. Common sense told him the craft had to be a helicopter, but it was a chopper unlike any he knew. Yet he saw no sign of spinning rotors, and a moment later, when the aircraft abruptly departed, it did so in the blink of an eye, accelerating from zero to an incredible speed faster than any copter ever made.

Percy found himself alone at the center of a sea of dead zombies. He blinked, inclined to believe he'd imagined the whole thing if not for the corpses ringing him.

Gunshots boomed at the farmhouse.

Spurred to action by the thought of Burroughs and the children still being under seige, Percy renewed his effort to extract his foot from the hole. He heaved and strained, and after a minute his leg popped free.

Grabbing the Franchi, he straightened and hurried toward the battle, grimacing at acute pain in his right leg. A sprain, he reasoned, and pressed onward.

A pack of white-shirts was gathered at the breached back door and attempting to gain entry. Evidently Seaman Burroughs had gone from the upstairs window to the head of the narrow hallway leading from the door to the kitchen, because from within the house came the thundering of his submachine gun and several of the crazies fell.

Ignoring the torment when he put pressure on his right foot, Percy came to the yard and bore down on the pack from the rear. He had to be careful not to let stray rounds penetrate the house or he might

18

identally hit Burroughs and the kids. Accordingly he angled to the right, to the corner of the building. Halting, he aimed at those nearest the doorway.

None of the creatures had as yet spotted him.

Percy grinned as he cut loose, the Franchi bucking in his hands. He killed half of them before the rest pivoted toward him, and he kept the trigger pressed down as they charged. Only two were left when the submachine gun went empty.

In the manner of an old-time gunfighter Percy let go of the Franchi and drew his Colts, the gleaming automatics up and out in the time it took the zombies to take a single stride. He shot each of them three times, going for the heart, rocking them on their heels. They fell side by side, one twitching and kicking for a bit before expiring.

From inside the house came more gunfire.

Percy holstered the pistols, retrieved the Franchi, and ran to the doorway. Hurrying toward him were three figures he recognized; Janet, Randy, and the stocky form of Tom Burroughs.

"John!" the eleven-year-old boy shouted.

"Come on," Percy urged, rapidly replacing the spent magazine.

The children emerged in a rush, Randy going a few yards and halting, his thirteen-year-old sister throwing herself at Percy and wrapping her arms around his midsection.

"Thank God you're here!" she wailed.

"Head for the barn," Percy told them, scanning the yard to make certain no white-shirt reinforcements were arriving. He saw Burroughs whirl and fire back down the hall and perceived pale pursuers at the far end.

Janet let go of the officer and ran with her brother toward the immense red barn twenty yards to the southwest.

19

Backpedaling after them, Percy yelled at the ⸏ man. "Forget about them, Tom. Let's go."

The blond Burroughs barreled outside and joined his superior officer. "They broke down the front door too. I didn't think you'd make it in time."

"I had help."

"Help?"

"I'll explain later. We've got to reach the car."

They sped to overtake the kids and did so just as the pair reached the enormous barn doors.

"I'll open them," Burroughs offered, slinging his Franchi over his left shoulder and gripping the edge of the left-hand door.

"Look!" Janet screeched, pointing at the house.

Percy swung around to see zombies spilling out the doorway and glancing in all directions. The leading white-shirts heard her cry and lumbered toward the barn. He unclipped a grenade, pulled the safety pin out, and executed an overhand toss, trying to plant it smack in the middle of the monstrosities.

True to his aim the grenade came down behind the foremost crazies. The explosion toppled them as if they were made of straw, slaying every one, including those just exiting the house.

Percy glanced at Burroughs, who was now working on the right-hand door, and gave him a hand.

"Hurry. Please hurry," Janet prompted, fidgeting nervously, terrified of being caught.

"Into the car," Percy instructed as he pushed the door wide. The siblings obeyed, getting in the passenger side, sliding into the rear seat. He reached into his front pocket for the keys and hastened to climb in behind the steering wheel.

Burroughs made it unanimous, sitting next to the officer and slamming his door shut. "Where to now?"

"Anywhere would be better than here," Percy responded, inserting the key into the ignition. With

20

a prayer that the engine would start, he turned it over.

The very walls vibrated as the Chevelle thundered to life.

"Behind us!" Randy warned.

Percy glanced into the rearview mirror to find a white-shirt directly behind the car, shuffling forward. "Hold on," he advised, shifting into reverse, and tramped on the gas pedal.

Unable to evade the vehicle, the zombie crumpled under its irresistible weight as the bumper caught him in the thighs and crushed both legs.

Percy felt a bump when one of the tires went over the ghoul, and then the car was out of the barn and there were more crazies on all sides. He braked, slapped the gearshift into drive, and spun the wheel furiously, shooting into the gap between the two buildings, making for the road in front of the house.

A pair of white-shirts barred the car's route.

His lips set in a grim line, Percy drove straight into them, seeing their arms outflung as they were plowed under the front end. Another bump and the Chevelle raced into the clear, slewing onto the front lawn.

"Go! Go!" Randy enthused.

Percy needed no encouragement. He hit the road doing forty, simultaneously tramping on the brake and turning the steering wheel, bringing the car level. The rear tires squealed mightily and burnt rubber as he accelerated, his adrenaline lending him the reflexes of a race car driver. As if shot from a cannon the car rocketed down the road to the northeast.

"We did it," Burroughs commented, elated.

"There's more of them," Janet declared, leaning forward to point to the right.

A half-dozen whitish scarecrows who had been moving toward the farmhouse were now trying to intercept the Chevelle.

Percy left them in the dust. The speedometer climbed to seventy, then eighty, and ninety, the landscape zipping past too quickly to be seen. He knew the next junction was two miles off and he entertained no intention of slowing before getting there.

"Where did all those white-shirts come from?" Seaman Burroughs wondered aloud.

"The countryside is crawling with them," Percy agreed. "It's like they came out of the ground."

"Don't ask me how they found us," Burroughs said. "We were waiting for you in an upstairs bedroom, talking softly, definitely not loud enough to be heard outside, and the next thing I knew there was a crazy in the doorway. I blew him away and ran downstairs to find the doors still locked and the windows still latched." He paused. "How could he have gotten in?"

"He couldn't," Percy said, his attention on the road. "Maybe he was hiding in the basement when we went in earlier."

"But I checked it."

"What happened after you shot him?"

"More started showing up outside and before long they were battering at the doors, trying to get in."

"But they didn't try to break out any windows?"

"No, sir."

"Dumb as bricks," Percy muttered, recalling the battle between the survivors in Argyle and the horde of white-shirts who eventually overran them. The zombies had attacked the survivors' stronghold for days before it occurred to them that instead of trying to break through the brick walls and the heavy iron gate surrounding the grounds they should go *over* the walls to gain entry.

"Did *Liberator* come?" Janet asked hopefully.

"Not yet," Percy answered, and heard her groan. "But the ship will arrive at the rendezvous soon. We can count on Captain Donovan."

22

"What if it arrives while we're gone?" Randy inquired. "Will your friends wait?"

"Certainly," Percy said, although the question sparked a worry. Sure, Donovan would wait, but for how long? He had to get back to the sound, an impossible task with the area infested by the unexpected influx of demented white-shirts.

"What did you mean back there about having help?" Burroughs inquired.

In detail the executive officer told about his own fight with the crazies and the timely arrival of the mystery aircraft.

"What could it have been?" Burroughs asked when his superior concluded.

"Your guess is as good as mine."

Randy spoke up. "Why did they help you and then leave?"

"I don't know," Percy admitted.

"We'll never be rescued," the boy said forlornly.

"Sure we will. Hang in there."

"We're tired of hanging in there," Janet said. "First our mom and dad were killed, then all those nice people in Argyle, and now it seems as if we'll never reach that wonderful island you've told us about." She pouted. "Why can't things go right for once?"

Percy didn't have an answer for that one.

The brother and sister leaned back in their seat, both trying bravely not to let their despair show, both signally failing.

In short order they came to the junction. Percy brought the Chevelle to a stop and gazed down each branch, debating which way to go. Uppermost in his mind was finding a way of safely reaching the appointed pickup point. He envisioned the sub surfacing in the middle of the sound and the crew spotting only white-shirts on the shore. Then it hit him. There hadn't been any on the shore itself.

Percy took a sharp right, smiling at an idea that gave them a fifty-fifty chance of achieving their goal.

"Where are we going?" Burroughs asked.

"To the northwest end of Saint Andrew Sound."

"Why there?"

"I think we can sneak back along the shore to the rendezvous site and—"

"But the zombies . . ." Burroughs interrupted in protest.

"There weren't any near the water. We know they can't swim, so under normal circumstances they must stay away from it," Percy speculated. "We made a mistake tonight. All of us should have been waiting at the sound."

"All of us waited all last night, sir," Burroughs noted, "and *Liberator* never showed up as the captain promised."

"That's right," Percy said, remembering that it had been his brainstorm to have the kids stay behind instead of going with him to the sound. He hadn't wanted them to spend another long, cold night fruitlessly waiting for the ship; he'd felt they would be safer and much more comfortable with the seaman guarding them at the farmhouse. So much for his bright ideas.

"Then why risk the danger again?"

Percy recognized that Burroughs was worried about the children, not either of them. "We'll take the inflatable out to the center of the sound," he proposed. "There's no way the white-shirts can get to us there." He frowned. "I should have thought of it sooner."

"What's an inflatable?" Janet interjected.

"Don't you know anything?" Randy responded before either of the men could explain. "An inflatable is a boat that you blow up like a balloon. I read about them in a book on the Navy."

"Is he right?" Janet asked.

24

"On the money," Percy confirmed, smiling. "We have one hidden on the south shore."

"Won't it take a long time to blow it up?"

"It's already inflated," Percy detailed. "We came ashore in it after *Liberator* dropped us off." He mechanically gazed into the rearview mirror, his calm expression transforming in a twinkling into one of sheer astonishment. For there, perhaps a quarter of a mile off, was a pair of headlights.

A vehicle was chasing the Chevelle.

### 3

Donovan became all business immediately. "Put them on the screen," he commanded.

"Feeding data into Cyclops now," Jennings said, punching buttons on his console.

A second later seven black blips materialized on the vivid holographic display, accurately positioned almost due north of the sub's current position. The blips quickly grew in size.

"Speed?" Donovan asked.

"One hundred and ten miles an hour."

"Sound Alert Stations."

The strident alarm blared to life, wailing throughout the length and width of the majestic ship, galvanizing the crew into mass action as men scrambled out of their bunks or raced from the galley or wherever else they happened to be toward their duty stations.

"Mr. Hooper, shallow dive. Keep our masts above water. I want our radar fully operational."

"Shallow dive it is, Captain."

Donovan watched as the icon representing *Liberator* eased just under the surface until only the top of her blister cleaved the surface. "Our speed?"

"Ten knots, sir."

"Bring us to twenty. Get us the hell out of here," Donovan ordered. He didn't like the idea of having the ship hemmed in by the relatively narrow confines of the James River. They had room to maneuver, but not enough to employ their maximum speed or take adequate evasive action should the incoming aircraft turn out to be hostile.

"Increasing speed to twenty knots," Hooper dutifully responded.

"Targets are decreasing theirs," Jennings announced. "Down to eighty miles per hour. Seventy. Sixty. Forty and holding steady."

On the screen the blips appeared to be warily nearing the submarine. They were evenly spaced in a tight line from east to west.

"The Cray-9 has configuration identification," Jennings stated. "They're choppers, Captain. Range slightly over ten miles."

"Are they the same type as the one we encountered off the coast of New Jersey?" Donovan inquired, remembering the brief scrap that ensued when an unidentified black helicopter streaked out of the blue and hovered nearby, its pilot refusing to answer *Liberator*'s hail. He had employed the lasers in the probe mode in an effort to learn more about the mystery aircraft, and the instant the blue-green lights struck the 'copter's cockpit the chopper had sped off. The ship's Cray-9 computer later analyzed the probe intel but was unable to supply any concrete information. The short laser contact had revealed the helicopter contained banks of ultrasophisticated equipment, including unknown weapons systems, and had been manned by four people, three men and a woman.

"Affirmative, sir."

"Hail them on all frequencies."

"Initiating hailing sequence."

Donovan studied Cyclops, noting a clear, straight stretch ahead. "Mr. Hooper, bring us to forty-five knots. Let's see if they intend to chase us."

"Yes, sir."

Half a minute went by.

"The targets are increasing speed to fifty miles per hour," Jennings said.

"Any response yet?" Donovan asked.

"Nothing but silence, Captain."

"Warn them to maintain their distance or we'll be forced to open fire."

"Here we go again," Alex declared.

Tense moments ensued as *Liberator* raced toward the mouth of the James and the helicopters continued to close in.

"They aren't bothering to acknowledge our warning," Jennings disclosed.

"Hardheaded bastards," Donovan muttered. What did they *want*? Who were they? He couldn't allow them to get much closer. If they were armed with missiles, which they undoubtedly were, every foot nearer they came geometrically increased the danger to the sub and the crew.

Jennings suddenly stiffened. "Captain, one of the helicopters has increased speed to ninety miles an hour and is heading straight for us."

"Lasers to weapons mode."

"Weapons Control activating both turrets."

Donovan had a decision to make. Should he let the chopper get within laser range, a mere 1,000 yards in the weapons mode, which was well under a mile, or should he take the aircraft out another way?

In addition to the lasers, *Liberator* sported several devastating offensive armaments. She carried dozens of Mark 70 long-range, laser-guided, acoustic-homing torpedoes with a range of 25,000 yards. She also had over twenty Mark 97N missiles, each tipped with a field-grade nuclear warhead. Her conventional weaponry was comprised of five Walther PB AutoStrafe machine guns. At a moment's notice any one of the big guns could be fitted to the special mount located aft of the topside bridge.

Since Donovan had no intention of surfacing to use a Walther and thereby exposing *Liberator* to possible enemy fire, and since torpedoes were notoriously ineffective against aircraft, his sole remaining option consisted of firing a Mark 97N. *Liberator* was far enough away to be spared from the effects of the limited nuclear blast, but he disliked the idea of expending one of the precious Mark 97Ns. For all he knew he might find a greater need for them later.

"Weapons Control reports we have laser lock on the target," Jennings said.

"Any acknowledgment yet from the helicopters?"

"None, sir."

"Tell Weapons Control to fire the second that bird is within range."

"Aye, Captain."

Alex leaned over the chair arm. "Don't," she said softly.

"What?"

"Don't open fire unless they do."

Mystified, Donovan looked at her, their noses almost touching. Her eyes accented the request more eloquently than her words. "You know I'm taking a risk as it is by letting that 'copter get within laser range."

"And you know that they could have shot a long-range missile at us by now if they wanted to."

"Maybe they don't have any."

"And maybe they're friendly."

"Then why the hell don't they answer us?"

"I don't know," Alex admitted, frowning, her gaze darting to the screen. "But my intuition is telling me that we should give them the benefit of the doubt."

"The benefit of the doubt could get us all killed."

"You're the commander. It's your decision."

"Thanks heaps," Donovan said testily, knowing full well she was right, his mind racing as he weighed the validity of her opinion and the likely consequences if he took her advice. Intuition was a tenuous factor at best, but there could be no denying its importance at critical moments when the difference between life and death often rested on an officer's gut instinct.

"Target is coming up on nine miles and continuing to close," Jennings revealed.

Donovan drummed his fingers on the chair arm while watching the holographic depiction of the lead aircraft and those farther behind it. What did his gut instinct tell him? he asked himself, and frankly conceded that if he had his choice he'd rather not take on the seven 'copters unless there was no other option. Not that he feared they might be able to cripple *Liberator*—which they might. But Alex had a point. Those choppers just might be potential friendlies who were as unsure of *Liberator* as he was of them.

"They still won't answer us, sir," Jennings reported.

"Keep trying right up to the last moment," Donovan said. He recalled again the previous encounter with a similar 'copter and inspiration struck. "Mr. Jennings, I've changed my mind. Switch the lasers to probe mode."

"Probe, Captain?"

"Are you hard of hearing?"

"No, sir. Probe mode it is."

"The last time we scared off one of these birds with a short laser burst," Donovan reminded him and the rest of the anxious bridge crew. "Let's see if we can avoid bloodshed this time with the same trick. Jennings, at five and a half miles rake that sucker from its nose to its tail."

"Yes, sir."

"And this time keep the lasers locked on it no matter what evasive action it takes."

"Will do."

30

"Captain, a partially submerged cargo ship ahead," Helmsman Hooper declared.

Annoyed at himself for not paying attention to the James River, Donovan stared at the hulk drifting slowly with the current and stated, "Reduce speed to thirty knots. Use your discretion and swing around it."

"Cutting back to thirty knots."

"Lead target is at one hundred and fifteen miles an hour and increasing speed," Jennings said. "Could be a strafing run."

"I'm aware of that," Donovan responded gruffly. The magnitude of the risk he was taking began to sink home. For an instant he felt tempted to change his mind once more.

"Thank you for not shooting it down," Alex whispered at that most timely of junctures.

"You're welcome."

"Eight miles out and flying at one hundred and twenty-five miles an hour," the communications officer detailed.

"Mr. Jennings, I want the computer to unscramble the lasers' incoming data instantaneously. Give me everything as you receive it."

"Understood, sir."

No one spoke for over a minute. The icons on the screen now truly resembled miniature streaking helicopters instead of vague blue-green blips.

"Range is just over six miles, Captain."

"Get ready."

"Six miles. Five-point-eight. Five-point-six."

"Fire!"

On the Cyclops display twin beams of bluish green light shot from *Liberator* and struck the oncoming aircraft head-on.

"A hit," Jennings verified. "The target is not—repeat, is *not*—taking evasive action."

Why not? Donovan mused, but had no time to ponder the strange behavior.

31

"The data is flashing onto the monitor," Jennings said, and started relaying the intelligence in short, clipped sentences, trying to keep up with the display. "Model, unknown. Configuration conforms to typical attack craft style. Various modifications evident." He paused. "Fuselage coated with black anti-infrared paint. Armor plating covers the lower third of the cockpit. Windscreen contains glazing compound. It has nine layers of hardened glass."

Donovan was riveted to every statement.

"Chopper fitted with an M199 cannon in the nose. Main rotor moving at five hundred twenty-four revolutions per minute."

One of the crewman knowledgeable about helicopters whistled in appreciation.

"Electronic equipment galore. Lasers have found an infrared jammer." Jennings glanced at Donovan. "Also evidence of a laser scrambling system."

"What?" Donovan said, straightening. "There is no such system."

"The computer begs to differ. Ceramic-coated source is located aft of the air intake," Jennings said. His voice acquired an edge. "It's on low power."

The revelation stunned Donovan. It meant whoever was on that 'copter was deliberately letting the aircraft be scanned. No wonder the pilot hadn't taken evasive action. But why were they allowing themselves to be probed?

"There's more, Captain," Jennings said. "Aft RWR antennas noted. VOR aerials present. Shape of undercarriages suggests presence of skids instead of wheels. The chopper also has stub wings."

"Missiles?"

"Nothing yet," Jennings replied, then promptly corrected himself. "Wait. Here we go. TOW launch tubes attached to each stub wing."

"That's all?"

"Nothing on missile type. Starboard and port rocket launchers also indicated."

32

"It's armed to the teeth," Donovan commented, noting the distance to the target on the screen. In a minute the chopper would be within weapons mode range. "Cease probe."

"Probe deactivated."

"Switch to weapons mode just in case," Donovan directed. Not that it would do much good until the helicopter came within a thousand yards of the sub.

"Switching."

Helmsman Hooper spoke up. "More garbage in the channel, sir."

"Reduce speed to twenty knots."

"Aye, Captain."

Communications Officer Jennings suddenly twisted a dial on his monitor. "Captain, they've activated a laser range finder in their nose. They have us locked in their missile sights."

Donovan came out of his chair, his pulse pounding. The sons of bitches were going to fire!

**4**

Half a world away, on the South Pacific island known as Espiritu, Donovan's younger brother, Charlie, stood on the beach and thoughtfully regarded the tracks imprinted in the soft sand at the water's edge. Clad in jeans and a blue T-shirt, he wore a Colt stainless steel government model .45 on his right hip and cradled a Franchi in his muscular arms.

"It's them, all right," commented his huge companion. "And those are fairly fresh."

Charlie nodded and glanced at the giant, the former professional wrestler who went by the name of Baltimore Jack, a bronzed titan whose strength equaled any three ordinary men, yet who possessed a heart and nature of the purest gold. They'd grown close during the weeks Tom had been gone and Charlie now rated Jack as one of his best friends. "Jenkins was right."

"We're lucky he spotted them when he came out here to go fishing," Jack remarked. As usual he wore a battered felt hat over his sandy hair, a tattered green T-shirt, and old khaki trousers that had been in their prime a decade ago, cut off at the knees. Instead of a gun he carried a makeshift club in his brawny left hand, a stout section of a thick branch he had whittled down until the bark was gone and then tapered at one end. The club lent him the aspect of a beachcombing Samson out to slay Philistines.

34

Or killer dogs.

Charlie squatted and studied the various tracks. "I'm no Daniel Boone, but I make it at least a dozen."

"We have our work cut out for us."

"Us?"

"You don't think I'm going to go back and leave you out here alone?" the wrestler said.

"I *am* chief gunnery officer," Charlie reminded him. "And Tom did leave me in charge of security on Espiritu until he returns."

Baltimore Jack crossed his massive arms and sighed. "Now don't start that garbage again. First of all, you're chief gunnery officer on *Liberator*, and I don't see her anywhere in sight. Second of all, I don't care if your brother appointed you island president. It doesn't mean diddly to me, brother."

"Have you no respect?" Charlie asked with a grin.

"Not for all that military hogwash. And political crap leaves me cold. One of the reasons I moved here shortly before the war was to get away from all that bogus power trip bullshit."

"You should have lived way back in the 1960s," Charlie mentioned, only partly in jest. "You would have made an excellent hippie."

"No way, dude. I wouldn't have gone in for all that free love jive."

"You wouldn't?" Charlie responded in surprise.

"No way, man. Free love is for animals and geeks who like to play Russian roulette with their bodies. I take too much pride in mine to risk getting a lousy social disease," the giant stated emphatically.

"You never cease to amaze me."

Jack grinned. "I'll take that as a compliment." He nodded at the tracks. "So what are we going to do, boss?"

Rising, Charlie stared at the western horizon. The sun would dip out of sight in an hour, ninety

minutes tops. Plenty of time remained for them t.
follow the tracks as far as they could, and all of
their effort would be more than justified if they
could only locate the lair of the man-eaters. The
thought brought a scowl to his face. Who would
have ever thought that *dogs* could be so vicious? But
then, the dogs he remembered so fondly were cod-
dled pets treated more like royalty than animals,
dogs whose affectionate natures had been developed during the course of the long evolutionary
companionship of humankind and the canine species in general.

These dogs, Charlie mused, were another matter entirely, feral canines living in the wild and
conditioned to kill anything remotely resembling
possible food. The theory went that centuries ago
European sailors, for whatever reason, had either
abandoned their pet dogs or given them as gifts
to the natives. Left to their own devices, the dogs
had reverted to a bestial state and were now the
dominant predators on the island—man excluded.
Already the current pack had been responsible for
two deaths, and Charlie intended to see to it that
they were exterminated before anyone else suffered
the grisly fate of being torn limb from limb.

Charlie turned and gazed in the direction of the
village, hearing the faint laughter of children and a
mother calling for her offspring, then surveyed the
rest of their Pacific wonderland.

Four miles wide and ten miles long, Espiritu's
shape was reminiscent of a figure eight that had
been laid on its side. The caldera of a long-extinct
volcano claimed the east end, rimmed by a wall
of ancient volcanic rock and coral. Millennia ago
the sea had poured into it, producing a seemingly
bottomless lake teeming with fish.

Occupying the very center of the island and ringed
by dense jungle was the former native village, now
inhabited by the survivors. Most of the huts had

36

been expanded and converted to reflect the Western life-styles of their new owners. A crude fence, recently erected, served as the first line of defense against the marauding dogs.

Towering two thousand feet above the west end of Espiritu loomed an active volcano, gray smoke curling skyward from its bubbling crater every hour of every day. More lush jungle encircled the base of the volcano except on the north side, where a sheer cliff reared half the height of the ominous cone.

From where Charlie was standing, on the broad beach at the northeast tip of the island, he watched the smoke pump aloft and wondered for the umpteenth time how they could have been crazy enough to settle next to a potential disaster. Oh, he knew that Alex's extensive computerized research indicated the volcano hadn't erupted in countless thousands of years and undoubtedly wouldn't for countless more. But he couldn't help recalling the old adage his darling great-grandmother had repeated with chronic regularity when he was a small boy, nearly every time he'd been in trouble: "Where there's smoke, there's fire."

Baltimore Jack coughed impatiently. "What's it going to be? Do we go after them?"

"We follow the tracks," Charlie confirmed, and turned westward. He wished he could go get the rest of his gunnery detail, but traveling to the village and returning would waste almost half of the daylight left. And since none of the other survivors were on the beach, Jack and Charlie were on their own. He hefted the Franchi and moved at a brisk clip, the giant at his side.

They took the same course as the pack, staying close to the water for hundreds of yards, then slanting into the jungle. Evidently the dogs were heading straight for the volcano.

Charlie's brow knit as he contemplated the smoking cauldron. Once before a trail of tracks had led

37

toward it, leading him to surmise the pack's lair was somewhere up there in one of the many caves known to dot the rocky, ash-covered terrain. Searching each and every one was out of the question until *Liberator* came back and more manpower became available.

"How's Betty doing?" Baltimore Jack unexpectedly inquired.

"What's it to you?" Charlie rejoined defensively.

"Whoa. Chill out, guy. Everyone on the island knows the two of you are a hot item. I was just making conversation."

"Pick another topic," Charlie said, feeling slightly foolish at making such an issue over an innocent remark, but he couldn't help himself. His relationship with Betty Thompson had reached the serious stage. The very serious stage. He'd even toyed with the notion of proposing, but realized he shouldn't rush things. She might not be ready yet.

Betty Thompson hailed from San Francisco. A former librarian, she'd lost her husband, a U.S. Marine, during the war. Now she resided in a hut on the north side of the village with her two children: eight-year-old Melanie, who regarded Charlie's courtship of her mother with as much enthusiasm as she would probably show while being consumed by cannibals, and six-year-old Stevie, who felt that, compared to his deceased dad, Charlie rated a Wimp-of-the-Year award.

"Sorry, pal," Baltimore Jack said, looking like a puppy that had just received a stern reprimand.

"I'm the one who should apologize," Charlie said. "I shouldn't have snapped at you."

"No harm done," the ex-wrestler said, and winked. "The two of you must be getting hot and heavy, huh?"

"I like her," Charlie admitted, in the same manner he might admit to liking spareribs.

"Come on. You can level with me, dude. When are you going to move in with her?"

"I thought you agreed to pick another topic."

Jack chuckled. "I never agreed to nothing."

Deciding that turnabout was indeed fair play, and hoping to change the subject whether the giant felt inclined or not, Charlie asked, "What about you?"

"Me? I don't have a main squeeze."

"Why not? I've seen some of the women giving you the eye."

"You have? Who?"

Charlie frantically tried to recall the name of any woman he had seen even so much as glance at his intimidating friend. "Oh, Joan Carlotti, for one."

"She did? Really?"

"Would I lie to you?"

"Gee. I'll have to ask her out sometime," Baltimore Jack proposed, genuinely pleased at the disclosure.

"Don't rush into anything," Charlie hastily advised, and laughed. "You know how women are."

"No, I don't."

"Come again?"

The ex-wrestler stared off into the distance. "I'm not a lady's man, dude. Around women I get all tongue-tied. You can count the number of dates I've had on one hand."

"You're exaggerating," Charlie stated, his eyes on the verdant terrain ahead.

"Nope. I'm afraid to even ask a woman out."

"A guy with your build?" Charlie responded skeptically, glancing at his friend.

"Believe it or not, many women don't go in for men with a lot of muscles. I figure they think we're all airheads who are only after one thing," Jack said rather sadly.

"Really?" Charlie said, not bothering to mention that he thought it would be the other way around. By all rights women should literally drool over guys who could flex a pinky and sprout a muscle the size of a watermelon. He'd always envied those weight lifters who gave the impression of being sculpted from stone but had never possessed the initiative to pump iron himself. Besides, the idea of all that sweating grossed him out.

"I had a girlfriend once," Jack revealed. "We went together for a whole year. Then one day she up and left me for an accountant." He paused. "She told me he stimulated her libido, not her salivary glands." He paused again. "To this day I don't know what the hell she meant by that. Do you?"

Charlie shook his head. "If I could understand women, I'd write a book and make a mint off the royalties."

"Too bad there's not many people left in the world to read it."

The comment reminded Charlie of his brother, out there somewhere trying to rescue a few survivors, and of the hardships they all faced trying to rebuild civilization from scratch.

"Look," Baltimore Jack said, stopping to point at a patch of exposed soil.

Clearly defined in the rich earth was a large paw print.

"We're still heading in the right direction," Charlie idly noted, pressing onward. All around them was abundant wildlife. Gaily plumed parrots flitted from branch to branch. Colorful creepers, fruit doves, and leaf birds winged blithely about. Monkeys dangled precariously from high limbs or perched in the crooks of trees and chattered their simian gossip. He found the animal sounds reassuring. If there were predators in the area, the creatures would clam up.

"I heard one of the colonists say yesterday that we should try to poison the dogs," Baltimore Jack mentioned. "What do you think?"

"It's a stupid idea. What's to stop other animals from eating the poison? Hunting the pack down will take longer, but at least we won't contaminate the entire food chain in the process."

The giant smiled. "I was hoping you'd say that."

They drew ever nearer to the smoldering volcano, its enormous cone dominating the landscape. Vegetation extended a third of the way up its slopes; above lay the rocky ground and the caves.

"There's my place," Jack said happily.

Charlie tilted his neck and spied the Swiss-style A-frame chalet situated on the south slope. Solar powered, with a windmill as a backup energy source, the house was the only residence on Espiritu that contained all of the conveniences and comforts of the prewar culture. Compared to most of the huts, the chalet was downright luxurious.

"When will you let me move back in?"

"When the dogs are destroyed."

"But that could take weeks, even months," Jack noted in disapproval.

"You can't live up there by yourself with feral canines on the loose."

"I lived here for a year before all of you showed up and never had any problems."

"Only because the dogs might not have considered a sole human as much of a threat to their territory. But now it's different. They've killed men. They have a taste for human flesh. You're not going back yet and that's final."

"How about if I only stay there during the day?"

Charlie halted and stared at the ex-wrestler. He opened his mouth to argue when a chilling sound wafted to his ears and checked the words on the tip of his tongue.

Eerily emanating from the vicinity of the volcano came the howling of the bloodthirsty pack.

**5**

"Good Lord!" Seaman Burroughs exclaimed upon noticing Percy's stunned expression and gazing out the rear window. "There's a car on our tail."

The children twisted excitedly.

"Who can it be?" Janet wondered.

"Think they're friendly?" Randy asked.

"There's no telling,"Percy said, debating his next move, his right foot burying the accelerator. He wasn't about to let whoever was back there catch up—not yet, anyway. Not until he had a better idea who it was. Since the white-shirts lacked sufficient intelligence to drive tricycles, let alone cars, the occupants must be normal survivors. Still, many survivors were violent in their own right, looters and scavengers who would shoot a person over a mere trifle. He had to find out who they were before making contact.

A sharp curve appeared ahead.

Percy braked enough to safely make the tight swing to the left, and as the Chevelle shot out onto a long straightaway he spied a darkened house bordered by a gravel driveway on the right. Instantly he slewed to a screeching stop, missing the turnoff by a dozen yards. Throwing the gearshift into reverse, he quickly backed into the driveway, stopped beside a hedge, and killed the headlights.

Randy laughed. "This is fun, sort of like hide-and-seek."

A potentially deadly hide-and-seek, Percy reflected, rolling down his window. He drew his right Colt and held it ready for prompt use.

All four of them sat perfectly still in expectant silence.

They didn't have long to wait. Soon headlights played over the curve and the roaring of an engine could be heard above the idling of their own. The car sped into sight the next moment, a sporty black two-door coupe manufactured by Toyo-Fordham, the company formed after the ailing American company was bought out by its Japanese counterpart in 2005. Both windows were down and as the coupe shot past the driveway loud rock music blared.

Percy counted three, possibly four people inside, two of them in the front. He heard loud laughter. Jutting from the passenger window was the barrel of a rifle or shotgun.

The coupe kept going, doing well over seventy.

"They didn't see us," Burroughs said in relief.

"What do we do now, Mr. Percy?" Janet inquired.

"We turn the tables," Percy said, placing the pistol in his lap. He pulled out, leaving the lights off, and sped in pursuit.

"Isn't this dangerous?" Janet mentioned.

"I can see the center line," Percy assured her. "If there are any obstacles on the road, the coupe will swerve and I'll have plenty of time to take evasive action."

"You hope," the girl said.

Deep down Percy knew her concern was justified, but he had to find out about those other people even at some small risk to their own safety. The coupe was still roaring into the night like the proverbial bat out of hell. If he stayed a hundred yards back it was doubtful the Chevelle would be discovered.

"They must be nuts," Burroughs remarked. "Why else would they go joyriding at night with white-

43

shirts roaming all over the landscape?"

"Actually, a car is one of the safer places to be," Percy disagreed. "The white-shirts have no way of stopping a vehicle. They haven't figured out how to erect barricades yet."

"Give them time and they will," Burroughs predicted.

They trailed the coupe through the inky, gloomy countryside, a rural area where few dwellings existed, for over five minutes. Not a light showed anywhere.

One of the newer luminescent road signs materialized on the right, informing them that Interstate Highway 95 lay a mile distant.

Immediately the coupe slowed.

Percy compensated accordingly, seeing the other car's taillights brighten briefly. A cluster of buildings on his side and a few hundred feet in front of them loomed like squat black boxes against the backdrop of the heavens.

The driver of the coupe wheeled off the road and into a spacious parking lot flanking the structures. He stopped and out the passenger side hopped a skinny man wearing a black leather jacket and jeans.

Braking abruptly, Percy turned off the ignition and saw the figure move away from the coupe and unzip his fly.

"What's that man doing?" Janet asked.

"Three guesses, dummy," her brother retorted.

Percy felt oddly embarrassed when the man proceeded to take a leak. He derived small comfort from the guy's being too far off to note details.

Janet giggled self-consciously and looked away.

To Percy's surprise, two other people emerged from the coupe, the driver and a young woman. They stretched while gazing all around. All three packed revolvers on their hips. He came to a hasty decision and opened his door. "Stay put until I get

44

back or signal for you to join me."

"What are you planning to do, sir?" Burroughs inquired.

"If I can get close enough to take them by surprise, we'll find out who they are," Percy said, and slid out, grabbing his Franchi before he straightened.

"Be careful," Burroughs said.

"Please," Janet added.

Dashing to the left, Percy padded to the shoulder. There was no sidewalk, only a shallow ditch for drainage purposes. He leaped across it and crouched. A few high bushes and trees along the edge of the road promised good cover. Grasping the submachine gun in both hands he moved toward the parking lot.

The trio were conversing near their car. The skinny guy reached inside and withdrew a six-pack that he shared with his companions.

Beer? Percy guessed. Maybe Burroughs was right after all. Only idiots would drive around looped out of their gourds, white-shirts or no. He kept vegetation between himself and the coupe until only a dozen yards remained. Squatting, he studied the survivors.

They were young, in their early twenties. The man wearing leather had dark brown hair. The driver had blond hair to his shoulders and wore a dark green sweater and brown pants. He had his left arm draped around the slim shoulders of the woman, a redhead whose yellow top and jeans were sculpted to her shapely contours.

Percy had to get closer before they took off. But how? He looked down and felt the ground with his left hand until his fingers closed on a small rock. When in doubt use the oldest trick in the book, he decided.

The dark-haired guy was chugging his brew.

Raising his left arm, Percy tossed the rock as far

as he could and heard it clatter on the asphalt well past the coupe. The trio dropped their beers and wheeled, their hands dropping to their revolvers, seeking the source of the noise.

Hoping they weren't trigger-happy, Percy rose and dashed toward them, the Franchi levelled. The blond man heard his footsteps first and spun, starting to draw, his reflexes incredibly swift. "Don't!" Percy commanded in his sternest tone, halting with his finger caressing the trigger. "You're dead if you do."

Fortunately the blond guy complied. The other two pivoted. Shock transfixed the trio. At last the blond man found his voice.

"Who are you, mister?"

"Executive Officer John Percy from the U.S.S. *Liberator*. Who are you?"

"I'm Duke," the blond guy said, and nodded at the redhead. "This is Maggie." He motioned at the man wearing the leather jacket. "That's Yuma." His accent was distinctly Southern.

"Move your hands away from your weapons," Percy directed.

Duke hesitated. "How do we know we can trust you?" he countered.

"If I'd wanted you dead I could have shot you and been done with it."

In the feeble combined light from the dashboard and the overhead bulb that emanated through the open car door, Duke's troubled expression reflected the dilemma he was wrestling with.

"I believe him," Maggie suddenly declared.

"Well, I don't," Yuma stated, his fingers inches from his revolver. "What's to stop this Yankee from blowin' us away the minute we lower our guard?"

"Use your pitiful excuse for a brain," Maggie said. "Look at the way this guy is dressed. Look at his gun, for crying out loud."

46

"Doesn't mean a thing," Yuma insisted, his beady eyes mirroring his distrust.

The one called Duke finally spoke. "Like hell it doesn't." He extended both hands, palms outward to show his peaceful intentions. "Okay, mister. We don't want no trouble if you don't."

Percy relaxed slightly. Yuma was still poised to draw, so he swung the Franchi to cover him. "What about you, moron? If you're going to draw, get it over with. But you'd be wise to consider that all I have to do is tap this trigger and you'll be cut in half."

Yuma glanced at the submachine gun's barrel, licked his lips, and let his arms go limp. "Hell, mister. You can't blame a guy for being careful."

"Are you some kind of soldier?" Maggie inquired.

"I'm in—" Percy began, and promptly corrected himself. "I *was* in the Navy, serving aboard a submarine when World War Three erupted."

"What are you doing here?" Duke asked.

"We came ashore to try and save survivors from the white-shirts," Percy said, giving them the bare essentials. Until he trusted them fully he wasn't about to divulge every detail.

"We?" Maggie repeated.

Percy ignored her. "Tell me about yourselves. How have you survived this long?"

"Just lucky, I guess," Duke said. "Maggie and I were in a cabin up in the Blue Ridge Mountains when the shit hit the fan. We didn't have a radio or nothing and had no idea the war had broke out until we came down two weeks later."

The woman nodded, then shuddered. "All we found were bodies and those zombies in white."

"And him?" Percy probed, pointing the Franchi at Yuma.

"We met up with him outside of Athens," Duke revealed. "Ever since we've been sort of drifting from one place to another, living off the canned food

47

we find and staying one step ahead of the freaks."

"Haven't you seen other survivors?"

"A few here and there," Duke disclosed. "Most run off at the sight of us. Others open fire with no cause whatsoever."

"The whole world has gone crazy," Maggie said solemnly.

"Tell me about it," Percy responded, and looked at their coupe. "Nice set of wheels."

"We picked it up at a dealership in Monroe, a small town east of what's left of Atlanta," Duke stated. "We try to avoid the big cities where possible because that's where most of the zombies stay."

"Most, but not all," Maggie stressed.

"I know," Percy said.

"We saw another car a while back and were chasing it but they gave us the slip," Duke explained, and cocked his head. "Hey, was that you?"

"Yep."

"You must be one slick driver. How'd you lose us?"

Rather than possibly offend them by relating the ease with which he'd done so, Percy shrugged and answered, "An old trick I learned."

"Are there others with you, Yankee?" Yuma questioned.

"A few," Percy admitted. He gazed at the nearby buildings and realized they were part of a factory complex. The sound must not be far off. "What are your plans?"

"To stay alive," Duke said.

"Are you tired of roaming all over the place with the white-shirts constantly after you?"

Maggie snickered. "What kind of dumb question is that? Of course."

"How would you like to settle down where there are no zombies, where you could live the rest of your lives in peace?"

The trio exchanged perplexed glances.

"What are you talkin' about?" Yuma snapped. "There is no such place."

"Wrong," Percy said, controlling his temper. He instinctively disliked the skinny man and was doing his best not to show it. "There's an island in the South Pacific where a number of survivors from San Francisco and elsewhere have relocated. There's plenty of food and the weather is always pleasant."

Duke took a step forward. "You could take us there?"

Percy nodded. "On *Liberator*. We're due to rendezvous with her soon. I'm sure my captain would welcome you aboard."

"It sounds too good to be true," Maggie said.

"It probably is," Yuma remarked. "For all we know this guy has some kind of trick up his sleeve. He could be jerking us around."

"For what reason?" Duke responded.

"How should I know?" Yuma said. "Maybe he wants to gain our trust, then blow us away."

"You have a suspicious nature, buddy," Percy declared bluntly.

"Damn straight, Yankee. It's how I stay alive."

The man had a point. If the situation were reversed, Percy might be equally skeptical. "Tell you what. Come with me to the rendezvous site and wait for the sub. Once she surfaces you can make up your minds about going along. Is that fair enough?"

Duke nodded and went to speak, but before so much as a single syllable could issue from his mouth a maniacal screech rent the night from the vicinity of the industrial complex and a band of white-shirts appeared around the corner of the nearest structure.

## 6

"Mr. Hooper, evasive action," Donovan bellowed. "Take us to the bottom of the river."

"Aye, Captain," the helmsman responded, starting to manipulate his controls.

"Captain," Communications Officer Jennings declared, "the 'copter's laser range finder has been deactivated."

Donovan stared intently at the icon representing the onrushing chopper. What the hell was going on? Why would they prime the damn thing, then back down? "Double-check."

"Already have, sir."

"Belay the evasive action," Donovan ordered. "All stop instead."

"All stop it will be, Captain."

Jennings was glued to his monitor. "The helicopter has slowed. Down to one hundred miles an hour. Eighty. Fifty. Twenty." He paused. "It's now hovering at three and a half miles out."

The sound of heavy footfalls made Donovan glance over his left shoulder to find Chief Engineer Smith approaching.

"What the hell is going on, Skipper?"

"I wish I knew, Flazy," Donovan replied, facing the screen again.

The portly career sailor halted and thoughtfully regarded Cyclops. "I've been following everything on the monitors."

50

Donovan absently nodded. There were monitors positioned at strategic spots throughout the sub; in corridors, at work spaces, in living quarters, wherever they were most likely to be seen. Fed from the communications station, they permitted the crew to keep abreast of whatever might be transpiring at any given moment. The decision to install real-time monitoring capabilities in all areas of the ship had been one of the most hotly contested when the designers initially proposed it. Several admirals had objected on the grounds the system might adversely affect the command structure by allowing the crew to second-guess the captain, but their objections had been overridden in the belief that each crew member had a legitimate stake in the operations of *Liberator* and deserved to be fully informed at all times.

"Any idea who they are?" Flazy asked.

"Nope. Those choppers are unlike any we have on file."

"Do you want me to get a crew on deck and mount a Walther?"

"Not yet. They're not displaying any hostility so we'll do the same," Donovan proposed.

Alex stepped forward to join them. "Care for my input?"

"I didn't appoint you as our science officer so you could kibitz," Donovan told her.

Opening her mouth as if to make a sharp retort, Alex glanced around the bridge and frowned instead. "I'll keep that in mind, sir," she said formally, and went on crisply. "It's just a guess, mind you, but maybe whoever is out there wanted to let you know they could open fire at any time and that they're deliberately refraining to demonstrate their good intentions."

The same possibility had occurred to Donovan. "Could be," he agreed, and stared at Jennings. "Are we still hailing them?"

"Yes, sir. And still no answer."

"Every frequency?"

"As you instructed."

"Including the classified channels assigned to COG?"

"Affirmative, Captain."

"What's COG?" Alex asked.

"It stands for Continuity of Government, the general title given to the U.S. government's top-secret plan for ensuring our political and military leaders could survive any global disaster," Donovan explained. "The oversight of the various operations was assigned to the Defense Mobilization Planning Systems Agency way back in the early 1980s."

"Do you think these helicopters are connected to this agency?"

"I doubt very much that they're Russian or German. Their flying range can't be that great. They must be linked to our government in some way," Donovan speculated.

"I hope so," Flazy said.

"What about that Mount Weather place you mentioned?" Alex brought up. "Could they be from there?"

"Possibly," was all Donovan would commit himself to say.

Situated in Virginia, Mount Weather had been one of about fifty top-secret command-and-control centers dotting the country, an incredibly huge underground complex able to house over one thousand people for several years. The cost of its construction had been a staggering one billion dollars. Contingency plans had called for the president and other specially designated leaders to be whisked from Washington, D.C., at a moment's notice to Mount Weather or other bunkers. All such sites were supposedly capable of withstanding all enemy strikes except a direct hit.

As if the network of costly bunkers for America's

leaders hadn't been enough, the U.S. government also developed NEACP, or Kneecap, as the program was more commonly known. The National Emergency Airborne Command Post had consisted of four Boeing 747s outfitted with state-of-the-art telecommunications equipment. One had always been kept in the air, while a second had stood by at Andrews Air Force Base, less than ten minutes from the White House by 'copter, ready to take the president or other appointed high-ranking individuals on board.

Donovan knew there had been other survival-oriented programs, but they had been classified For Eyes Only, well above his access level. He'd heard rumors over the years, none of which could be substantiated. In toto, the existence of Mount Weather, Kneecap, and the varied other programs led to the inevitable conclusion that *some* leaders must have survived. If so, where the hell were they?

"Captain!" Jennings declared excitedly. "They're finally answering."

"Put it on the speakers," Donovan instructed. He wanted the entire crew to hear the exchange.

The communications officer flicked a toggle switch.

"—to U.S.S. *Liberator*, please acknowledge and confirm your identity. Again, this is Captain Drew Rockwood, Site R Security, requesting acknowledgment and confirmation. Over."

Feeling his stomach muscles involuntarily tighten, Donovan stepped quickly to the communications station with Alex and Flazy right behind him. "Give me a mike, Dave."

Jennings handed one over.

"Here goes nothing," Donovan said softly, and pressed the switch to transmit. "This is Captain Tom Donovan, U.S.S. *Liberator*. We copy. Over."

Faint static crackled from the speaker for a moment.

"Captain Donovan, I apologize for the delay in answering. But we're still not convinced that you are who you claim to be. I'd like to ask you a few questions. Over."

Donovan did a double take and glanced at Jennings, who appeared equally mystified. "What kind of questions?"

"Basic ones which only the real Donovan should be able to answer," Rockwood said. "For instance, what did your father do for a living?"

The query sparked painful memories and Donovan felt a twinge of resentment. He still had a hard time accepting the loss of his parents and didn't like being reminded of them. "He was a New York City police detective. Over."

"Correct. And your brother's name?"

"Charlie."

"The wharf where your father's boat was berthed?"

Donovan was stunned. "How the hell do you know my father had a boat?"

"Just answer the question, if you please," Captain Rockwood said.

"My dad's sailboat was kept at the Seventy-ninth Street boat basin in New York City."

"So far, so good. How old were you when you considered entering the priesthood?"

The question, revealing as it did an intimate knowledge of Donovan's background, a knowledge few people outside his immediate family had ever known, brought an upwelling of intense anger. "How did you know about that?"

"Please simply answer the question."

"Like hell I will, Rockwood," Donovan snapped. "I've had enough of this bullshit. You seem to know everything there is to know about me and I know nothing about you." He paused, feeling Alex's hand brush his elbow in reassurance. "What purpose does this interrogation serve?"

"I thought I'd already made that clear, Captain Donovan," Rockwood stated stiffly. "To confirm your identity."

"Why don't we arrange a meeting and you can confirm my identity in person? Over."

"No can do, Captain. We can't afford to let ourselves be suckered into a trap. Although I'm ninety-five percent convinced you are who you say you are and the sub you're on is indeed *Liberator*, I'm under strict orders not to risk losing any of the aircraft or men under my command."

"I can appreciate your caution," Donovan said. "I feel the same way about you. But if you know anything at all about the ship I command, then you're aware that she's unique. One close-up look should suffice to convince you."

"Incorrect, Captain," Rockwood replied. "*Liberator* is not unique. There is also the *Deutschland*."

"The what?"

"Do you mean to tell me that you don't know about *Liberator*'s twin, the nuclear sub built by Germany prior to the war?"

Comprehension dawned and Donovan blurted, "*Nemesis*."

"What?"

"You must be referring to the sub we sank," Donovan said, the memories returning in a rush.

*Liberator* had initially encountered the mystery sub subsequently dubbed *Nemesis* by the crew shortly after World War Three concluded. A series of indecisive engagements followed with neither ship gaining the advantage.

From scientific and technical journals, including the specs on all American warships of the late twentieth century and every bit of information on file concerning foreign navies, as well as pertinent reports in *Jane's Fighting Ships* and elsewhere, Donovan had been able to piece together the clues to the strange sub's origin.

*Liberator*, the first of the Omega-class subs, had never been meant to be the last. The keel and partial hull of a second prototype had been constructed, then scrapped when Congress refused to appropriate the required funds to finish the job. The Navy, eager to recoup its investment, sold the keel and hull to the Greater Germany Defense Force, or GDF.

Germany then moved the second prototype to a leased shipyard at Gdansk and publicly proclaimed its intention of building an entire fleet of nuclear attack submarines to contribute its fair share to the stabilization of the world in the postsuperpower era.

Then the hard-liners had returned to power in the Soviet Union and the European economy collapsed. Unable to build its fleet, the GDF stopped leasing the shipyard and nothing more was heard of Germany's plan to build her own Omega-class submarines. Western intelligence agencies were unable to determine if the GDF had finished constructing the first one, thanks to the GDF's advanced satellite jamming that prevented surveillance from being conducted at Gdansk. Rumors surfaced that the keel and hull had been destroyed in a fire, and since the sub was never observed or photographed its existence was discounted.

Only well after the war was Donovan able to uncover the truth.

Not only had the GDF built its prized sub, it had used it to start World War Three. The strategy had been deceptively simple.

Relations between the United States and Russia had grown increasingly hostile after the hard-liners took control. A series of minor confrontations led to a summit meeting of the Western powers in the Sea of Japan at which the leaders hoped to formulate an effective policy for opposing Soviet expansionism. And then, while the Western heads of state were gathered on an aircraft carrier for their conference, the GDF struck.

Charlie Donovan had been the Technician First Class serving on an HH-2G LAMPS helicopter patrolling the icy waters of the Bering Strait when the mystery sub streaked past to the south and launched a cruise missile at the aircraft carrier. The chopper was caught in the wash and went down.

With unerring accuracy the cruise missile obliterated the aircraft carrier and the Western leaders in one fell swoop. Naturally the rest of the world blamed the Soviets, who naturally denied committing the atrocity, and in no time at all the war of words naturally became the real McCoy.

Germany had masterminded the coup of the century, perhaps of the era, by provoking the two sides into almost destroying themselves, leaving the GDF to pick up the pieces and assume domination of the globe. The plan might have succeeded, too, if not for *Liberator*.

"You sank the *Deutschland*?" Rockwood asked in surprise.

"We sank a sub very much like our own," Donovan confirmed. "Since we didn't know its name, we called it *Nemesis*."

"This is wonderful news, if true," Rockwood said, excitement in his tone. "I must report this to my superiors."

"And what about us? Over."

Static hissed for half a minute.

"I'll tell you what. Do you know where Blakistone Island is in the Potomac River? Over."

"It rings a vague bell. Why?"

"Be there tomorrow at noon and all your questions will be answered."

"Now hold on," Donovan said, thinking of Percy and the further delay it would mean in reaching him. Before he could elaborate, Rockwood threw down the gauntlet.

"If you're who you claim to be and not some clever member of the Fourth Reich trying to lure us into a trap, then you'll show up at noon. Rockwood out."

"Wait—" Donovan said.

Again the speakers crackled with static.

"It's no good, Captain," Jennings stated. "The choppers are moving off rapidly. They're already at ninety miles an hour. Make that a hundred."

Donovan handed the mike back and summed up his commingled frustration and fascination with a single word. "Damn."

7

"Come on!" Charlie shouted, and took off toward the volcano at full speed, skirting the thicker undergrowth, the Franchi tightly grasped in both hands.

"Wait for me," Baltimore Jack declared, following.

But Charlie wasn't about to slow down for any reason. He could still vividly recall the two unfortunates who had been ripped to pieces by the pack and he wouldn't pass up any opportunity to return the favor. In addition, the intimidating burden of being responsible for the life of every colonist on Espiritu weighed heavily on his shoulders. The survivors were depending on him to take care of the man-eaters and he wouldn't let them down.

The howling continued, clearly coming from the northeast base of the smoking cone.

What were the dogs up to now? Charlie wondered, slowing as he drew nearer, not wanting to blunder onto them and give them the advantage. He pulled back the submachine gun's cocking handle and moved stealthily through the jungle until he glimpsed movement ahead. Instantly he froze.

Several canine forms appeared, moving rapidly from south to north in single file, too far off for a certain shot.

Charlie remembered his previous confrontation with the pack when they treed a couple of young boys. Their inherent viciousness had stunned him.

Just because they were dogs didn't mean they should be taken lightly. Their savagery knew no bounds and their strong, razor-sharp teeth could crush a human bone in a single bite. He had to be careful.

The last of the pack disappeared.

Advancing swiftly, the soles of his shoes making little noise on the dank carpet of grass underfoot, Charlie slanted toward the spot where he'd seen them. He glanced back once and saw no sign of Baltimore Jack.

At a small clearing ringed by trees on the west side Charlie found the tracks of the animals. Kneeling, he examined the prints, trying to determine how many dogs had passed by. As he touched the fingers of his left hand to the soft soil he heard a sound that chilled his soul.

From his rear came a low, throaty growl.

Charlie didn't bother standing and turning to ascertain the source. He automatically knew. At the first note of the feral challenge he threw himself to the left onto his back and twisted, his finger curling around the Franchi's trigger.

Its lips curled back to expose its wicked teeth, a dog hurtled out of the brush. As with most adult members of the pack, this one was the size of a German shepherd with a stocky body, short, powerful legs, and a long, bushy tail. Its thin coat was brown, the hair bristly and grimy.

Charlie took all this in at a glance, saw the dog spring, and fired, the recoil slapping the Franchi's stock against his right side.

Struck in midair, the wild dog was slammed to the ground by the dozen rounds that bored through its body. It tried to rise, to attack again, its paws desperately digging into the earth but unable to find a purchase.

In a smooth motion Charlie shoved upright and trained the weapon on the dog. Only then did he realize that sores dotted its body from head to tail and there were many bare patches where hair had once grown. The thing must be diseased. He put it out of its misery with a short burst, then scanned the vegetation for others.

A crashing of limbs announced the arrival of Baltimore Jack, who burst into the clearing and stood glaring madly about, ready to take on all comers. His gaze alighted on the dog. "Are you all right?"

"Fine. Just one jumped me."

Jack came over and studied the body. "It's in pitiful condition. Do you think the rest are the same way?"

The possibility hadn't occurred to Charlie. He stared at the dog, the germ of an idea taking root. Could the disease have anything to do with the pack's almost rabid behavior? "There's no telling," he said.

"Those shots probably scared the rest off. Do we keep going?"

"We sure do," Charlie confirmed, and headed in the direction the dogs had taken.

"Try not to make like the Flash this time," Baltimore Jack chided him.

They hiked along the base of the volcano until they came within sight of the high cliff bordering its north side.

"No sign of them, as usual," Jack remarked. "How can they vanish into thin air?"

"They can't," Charlie said, and paused to mop his brow. He idly surveyed the cliff face and nearly dropped the Franchi in surprise.

Moving up the supposedly sheer precipice were nine or ten dogs, strung out in a row behind the huge leader, the alpha, the dominant male. They glanced neither right nor left, only at whatever trail they were using, if indeed they were using one. From a distance it appeared as if they were walking on the vertical face itself.

61

"Jack," Charlie said, and pointed.

"Son of a bitch," the ex-wrestler blurted. "How are they doing that?"

"Let's find out," Charlie suggested, continuing northward.

By the time the two men reached the bottom of the rocky height, the dogs were close to the top.

Charlie craned his neck, watching the canines climb over the rim onto the top. Suddenly so much made sense. Now he understood how the pack could conduct its hit-and-run raids and dissolve into thin air. No one would have thought the dogs had their lair way up there. For that matter, no one knew what lay at the top since none of the survivors had been foolhardy enough to attempt to scale the steep face.

"Where's a helicopter when you need one?" Baltimore Jack joked.

Running his eyes down the cliff, Charlie discovered a narrow, serpentine path that led from the bottom to the pinnacle. At many points the path was no wider than six or seven inches, barely enough for a mountain goat let alone a dog. He marveled at their ability and reminded himself that necessity was often the midwife of extraordinary acts. If the dogs had been ruthlessly hunted by the natives, the pack would have been forced to seek out the most inaccessible locale on the island for its retreat. And except for the interior of the volcano, no spot was more inaccessible than the upper reaches of the imposing precipice.

"How are we going to get up there?"

"Do you know anyone who owns a hang glider?"

The giant laughed and rested his club on his brawny left shoulder. "Nope. Maybe we could build a catapult and shoot you to the top."

Charlie moved slowly along the bottom, seeking an alternate route. None existed.

"You know, I just had an idea," Jack said.

"Uh-oh."

"I'm serious."

"Okay. I know I'll regret this, but let me hear it."

"Why don't we try to take the dogs alive?"

Stopping, Charlie looked at his friend. "Did you bump into a tree when you were running through the jungle?"

This time the ex-wrestler didn't laugh. "They're just dogs. They don't know any better. Why wipe them out?"

"Because they're also killers."

"Not by nature. Not like jaguars or tigers or lions."

"And since when did you become an animal expert?" Charlie asked, amazed that the titan had proposed such a crazy notion. "These dogs have been roaming wild on Espiritu all their lives. For probably dozens of generations their ancestors have done the same. They've totally reverted to their basic predatory nature and trying to capture and domesticate them would be a monumental waste of our time."

"They deserve the chance."

"It's impossible. Forget it," Charlie advised, and went to continue. Baltimore Jack, however, pressed the issue.

"What's impossible about it? We're supposed to be smarter than a pack of measly dogs, aren't we? Why don't we use our superior intellect to solve the problem without exterminating them?"

Charlie was impressed by the intense sincerity etched in his friend's face. "Look, Jack, I know that despite your reputation as a rough-and-tumble wrestler you're a pussycat at heart. You like kids and puppy dogs and you wouldn't harm a fly if it landed on your food, but there *is* such a thing as going overboard, and in this case that's exactly what you're doing."

63

Baltimore Jack gazed wistfully at the cliff. "Maybe you're right. But I have to stick by my convictions." He expelled a long, drawn-out sigh. "I was just hoping we could do it differently this time."

"What are you talking about?"

"The world. I was hoping we'd learned from our mistakes."

Charlie walked to a nearby waist-high boulder and took a seat. "Okay. I can take a hint. Knowing how stubborn you can be, I know you won't let this drop until I hear you out. So go ahead. Enlighten me. Explain."

The ex-wrestler motioned with his huge right arm, encompassing all of Espiritu in a wide sweep. "One of the reasons I came here was to get away from the madness of the so-called real world. You know how bad it was."

From the top of the cliff wafted a faint howl.

"Overpopulation in the Third World countries had people living in disgusting poverty, packed together like sardines and fighting for grains of rice to stay alive. I saw it with my own eyes on the promotional tours we took to Mexico, Brazil, and elsewhere," Baltimore Jack said.

Charlie listened attentively. He'd seen some of the same nightmarish conditions himself.

"Pollution had gotten so bad that certain portions of the oceans were designated as contaminated zones, lawmakers in the U.S. were seriously thinking about turning a third of Nevada into one giant landfill, and students in Los Angeles and other metro areas were given oxygen masks at the start of each school year as standard school supplies," Jack mentioned.

"Yeah, I remember what it was like," Charlie said, bothered by the memories. He'd forgotten all about the miserable state of the poor planet at the time the war broke out. All he tended to remember were the pleasant aspects of prewar existence. Why was that? he wondered.

"The way I see it," Jack declared, "the war sort of wiped the slate clean. It sure as hell took care of the population problem. And in a perverse sort of way it made the whole pollution matter moot because now practically the whole world is in the same boat. It'll take thousands of years before things return to normal, if they ever do."

"What does all of this have to do with the dog pack?"

"I'm getting to that," Jack said. "Since the slate has been wiped clean, don't we owe it to ourselves to do things differently this time around? I mean, instead of acting like gods, of setting ourselves up as the lords and masters of the whole damned planet, shouldn't we learn how to live in harmony with Nature? Instead of treating animals as inferior creatures, shouldn't we treat them with the respect all living beings deserve?"

The passion in the giant's voice surprised and amused Charlie. "I had no idea you felt this way."

"What do you expect me to do? Waltz around carrying a sign like those animal rights activists used to do? I'd look silly as all get out."

"True," Charlie conceded.

Baltimore Jack stepped closer. "All I'm asking is for you to give my idea proper consideration. Think about it for a while before you tell me no."

"I will," Charlie promised, and scanned the cliff face. "But let's suppose for the sake of argument that I decide to go along with your harebrained scheme. How do you propose to capture the dogs and keep them docile long enough to domesticate them, or at least make them friendly?"

"I don't know," Jack admitted. "I'm hoping you'll come up with a bright idea."

"Me? I'd like to blow every last one of the dogs away."

65

"See? That attitude was so typical back in the old days. People weren't willing to take the time and energy to solve their problems. They either avoided them or stomped them into the dirt."

Thoughtfully chewing on his lower lip, Charlie looked up at the rim far above. "Maybe I should call a meeting of all the colonists and put it to a vote."

"It couldn't hurt," Jack said.

Charlie stood and studied the trail winding to the top. "And you know, there just might be a way to capture the dogs with a minimum of hassle."

"How?"

"That trail," Charlie said, nodding at the cliff. "If it's the only way up and down, then we might be able to rig a trap of some kind. Maybe dig a deep pit and cover it with grasses."

Baltimore Jack beamed. "I knew I could count on you."

"Don't get your hopes up. I'm just throwing out crazy ideas."

"Yeah, but once you put your mind to something you don't let up. Those dogs are as good as caught."

"I wish *I* had your confidence in me."

The ex-wrestler came over and clapped Charlie on the back. "You just keep thinking, little buddy. You'll come up with something."

"I'd better. In the meantime I'll post guards at the base of the cliff. If the dogs try to descend a few shots should discourage them. Maybe we can keep them penned up there until we figure out what to do."

"Excellent idea, dude. And I'll see what I can do about rustling up a hang glider."

Thinking that his friend was joking, Charlie laughed.

8

"Oh, God," Maggie said, pressing a hand to her throat. "More of those things."

"I hate those suckers," Yuma declared, and impulsively drew his revolver. He snapped off three hasty shots at the band but none of the white-shirts fell.

"You idiot," Duke stated angrily. "You've wasted more ammo."

Percy was tempted to fire himself but the zombies were over thirty yards away. He'd rather haul butt. "Get in your car and meet us on the road. You can follow us to Saint Andrew Sound," he proposed, and went to turn.

"Why the hell should we do what you say?" Yuma responded.

"Do whatever you want," Percy said. "It's no skin off my nose." Wheeling, he ran toward the Chevelle and heard Duke angrily address Yuma.

"That guy is our ticket out of this madhouse. Don't mouth off at him again."

"But how do we know we can trust him?" Yuma protested.

And then Percy was out of hearing range. He sprinted around a tree, then a shrub, angling toward the Chevy, eager to get inside where the white-shirts couldn't touch him.

Off to the right a pale figure materialized.

Where did they all come from? Percy wondered, and skirted a shoulder-high bush. Too late he saw the short apparition garbed in white standing directly in his path. With a gasp of horror he slammed into it. They both went down and he dropped the Franchi.

Frantically Percy scrambled to his knees, his breath catching in his throat at the sight of a zombie pushing itself off the ground not two feet away, a mere boy of fourteen or fifteen. The crazy saw him and reached out, mouthing a ghoulish hiss. Sheer loathing made Percy recoil and push to his feet. The submachine gun was lying right beside the white-shirt. He tried to lunge for it but the creature snatched at his wrist and he barely pulled away in time.

Keenly aware he had to get out of there, Percy did the unthinkable. He made bodily contact, his right foot flicking up and out and catching the white-shirt full on the face, his intent being to knock the thing down so he could retrieve his weapon. But in his state of fearful excitement he forgot the white-shirts were little more than animated corpses, mindless bodies kept alive by whatever disease produced the terrible condition.

It was as if he'd kicked brittle clay. The heel of Percy's boot met slight resistance, crushing the nose and driving deep into the crazy's face, buckling the face in upon itself.

Appalled, Percy drew his foot back and was disgusted to see gore and slime clinging to his shoe. A ragged hole now existed where the white-shirt's nose, mouth, and right eye had been. The thing keeled over backwards and twitched once before going limp. Quickly Percy scooped up the Franchi and continued his flight. Bitter bile rose in his throat and he suppressed an impulse to heave. A profoundly distressing thought echoed over and over in his mind: I've killed a boy!

Seaman Burroughs spotted him approaching and shoved the driver's door wide open.

Percy glanced over his right shoulder. The coupe was pulling onto the road up ahead. He came to the Chevelle, slid in, and handed the Franchi to Burroughs.

"What happened?" the crewman asked.

"I'll fill you in after we get out of here," Percy said, slamming his door, gunning the engine, and flicking on the headlights. He shifted and the Chevy leaped forward, the tires squealing, covering the hundred yards in no time.

White-shirts were advancing across the parking lot.

Percy braked sharply, stopping alongside the coupe. Duke was at the wheel again, Yuma beside him and glaring resentfully at the Chevelle. Maggie sat in the back.

"Lead the way, man," Duke called out.

Nodding, Percy accelerated to sixty in half as many seconds and let the speed continue to build.

"Who are those people?" Janet inquired.

"That one guy looked ticked off," Randy added.

With the zombies to their rear and the road in front of them clear, Percy let himself relax and spent a minute detailing the little he knew about the trio.

Janet was excited. "Do you really think they'll come with us to your island?"

"It's not *my* island," Percy said with a grin. "And yes, I think Duke and Maggie will go with us, but I'm not so certain about Yuma."

"The captain should be pleased," Burroughs commented.

"Yep," Percy agreed. Donovan wanted to increase the number of colonists on Espiritu to approximately two hundred, which Alex and her brother had determined was the optimum population the island could support without stressing the ecosystem. She was very keen on preserving the environment no matter what sacrifices might be entailed. In Percy's estimation Alex was too gung-ho in that respect. Although, since Espiritu was one of the few places on earth not tainted in any way by the war and must serve as their home for generations to come, Alex's zeal made practical sense.

"What if the submarine doesn't wait for us?" Janet unexpectedly asked.

"It will," Percy assured her.

"Our captain won't leave without us," Burroughs confirmed.

In due course they came to Interstate 95, which Percy refused to take. He much preferred the back roads, where there was less chance of running into the zombies or obstructions such as abandoned vehicles. In a quarter of a mile he found a side road leading toward the sound and took it.

"Mr. Percy?" Janet spoke up.

"Call me John," Percy told her. "What is it?"

"Will we have any say in who our new parents will be?"

Percy had never realized that kids asked so many questions, often completely out of left field. He'd promised them there would be couples on Espiritu willing to take them in.

"Sure you will," he answered. "You won't have to live with anyone you don't like."

"Will we be separated?"

"No," Percy said, hoping he was right. The colonists had no official adoption policy. He really didn't know how it would be handled. Taking in the Williams children would be a first.

In the distance buildings appeared. Beyond them, faintly visible, lay the glassy surface of Saint Andrew Sound.

Burroughs took a map from his pocket and used

a pencil flashlight to study it. "The nearest town is called Brunswick, located about five miles northwest of here."

"What about them?" Percy asked, and nodded at some buildings that had appeared ahead of them.

"Maybe a small settlement, sir. There's nothing listed on the map."

Percy looked in the rearview mirror at the coupe. Duke was staying six car lengths behind, allowing ample space to stop in an emergency.

"Hey, look at that!" Randy exclaimed.

"What?" Percy said, starting to twist his head, when he saw it himself. Off to the northwest, about where Brunswick should be, a bright circle of yellow light mushroomed in the sky and slowly drifted toward the ground.

"It's a UFO!" Janet declared.

"It's a flare," Percy corrected her, perplexed. None of the white-shirts could operate a flare gun. Survivors must be trying to send a signal of some kind. But to whom? And for what purpose? He braked and brought the car to a stop on the left side of the road, watching the flare settle even lower.

"What do you make of it, sir?" Burroughs inquired.

"I haven't the foggiest," Percy answered. He heard the coupe's engine and glanced to the right past the crewman as Duke drew to a stop next to the Chevelle.

"Isn't that a flare of some kind?" Duke shouted.

Burroughs rolled down his window so Percy could respond without having to yell.

"It sure is," the executive officer replied.

"We've seen them before," Duke revealed.

"You have? Where?"

"Oh, all over the place," Duke said. "Every few nights or so we've seen them, usually in the distance, and usually near a town or city. Those flares just come floating down out of nowhere. A few times

71

we went to investigate but by the time we got to where we thought the flares landed, they'd gone out and we couldn't find them."

Percy's brow furrowed as he pondered the implications. "I take it you've always seen them at night, never during the day?"

Duke turned and spoke to Maggie and Yuma, then faced the Chevelle. "Yeah. Only at night. What does it mean?"

"I'm not sure," Percy said, gazing to the northwest where the flare was almost out of sight below the tops of far-off trees. The idea of a single survivor or a group of survivors traveling all over the countryside and regularly shooting up flares was ridiculous. In the first place, whoever was responsible would need access to enough flares to fill a warehouse. And in the second place, even if the flares were being used to try to attract other survivors, it made no sense since the bright lights undoubtedly attracted white-shirts by the score as well. The practice defeated its own purpose.

Janet leaned forward. "Shouldn't we go see what's going on?"

Before Percy could express his opinion, Duke interjected a question.

"Hey, do you have kids in there, dude?"

"Yes," Percy said.

Seaman Burroughs added, "We saved them from the white-shirts and they want to go back with us."

Percy saw Duke say something to Yuma, and both Duke and Maggie laughed heartily. He imagined they were razzing their companion over his unfounded distrust. After all, someone who rescued children couldn't be all bad.

"The light went out," Randy declared.

Only stars now twinkled above Brunswick. Percy regarded the heavens solemnly, then swept the others with a meaningful stare. "We don't have the time to spare to go check on that flare. Our sub

...ght be waiting for us right this minute. I think we should keep on going."

"No argument here," Duke said. "We can't wait to get away from the zombies."

Letting up on the brake, Percy resumed driving toward Saint Andrew Sound. The buildings ahead worried him. Where there were dwellings there were usually white-shirts. He stuck to the middle of the road, giving himself room to maneuver should crazies come at him from either side.

The coupe stayed four car lengths to the rear.

A house appeared on the right, then another on the left. Both were dark inside, their doors and windows closed.

"What's that?" Janet suddenly cried, pointing.

A small animal darted onto the roadway thirty yards to the north and paused for an instant to look at the cars. Caught in the Chevelle's headlights, its slanted eyes glowed.

"It's a black cat!" Randy declared.

Percy slowed, not wanting to run it over, delighted at the discovery. This was the first cat he'd seen since coming ashore. An observation that once would have hardly merited attention now produced an odd sense of kindred empathy. The cat was a fellow survivor. It had endured the holocaust without being afflicted by the—

"What's it doing?" Janet asked in alarm.

The cat was hissing, arching its spine, and swatting at the approaching vehicles, a feline Saint George about to do battle with mechanized dragons.

"Oh, no," Burroughs said.

Frowning, Percy angled to the right side of the road, thinking of the children, trying to swing around the cat without mishap.

The tabby had other ideas. It abruptly charged.

"That thing is nuts!" Randy said.

"It has the radiation madness," Percy informed the boy, recalling the buck that had tried to ram

the car when Burroughs and he had been en rou̇ṫ
to Argyle. Then there had been the wolves in San
Francisco, the jaguars in Central America, sharks
everywhere in the Pacific, and even a flock of sea
gulls that had tried to peck the eyes from *Liberator*'s topside bridge crew. It was as if practically all
wildlife on the planet had risen in revolt against
humanity, as if the animals instinctively knew who
to blame for the destruction of their world and were
trying to get their revenge by exterminating the
so-called higher species responsible.

"Don't hit it," Janet wailed.

Spinning the steering wheel to the left, Percy
almost succeeded. But the determined cat leaped
straight at the grill and the resultant loud thump
left no doubt as to the outcome. He glanced into the
mirror and spied the small, limp black figure lying
near the center line.

"Darn it," Randy said. "Even the stupid cats are
wacko. I'll never own a pet again."

Janet bowed her chin. "I wish I would wake up
and find all of this has been a dream. A real *bad*
dream."

Driving down the middle of the road again, Percy
didn't know what he could possibly say that would
ease their suffering. They'd already lost their parents and nearly been killed by white-shirts. Left on
their own they wouldn't last very long. They were
orphans trapped in a lunatic asylum and he didn't
envy them one bit.

Burroughs placed a hand on the dash and peered
out the windshield. "Did you just see something?"
he asked, gazing upward.

"No," Percy replied.

"I thought I did."

No sooner were the words out of the seaman's
mouth than the interior of the car became bathed in
an excruciatingly brilliant burst of light and Janet
screamed in terror.

Donovan held the brainstorming session in *Liberator*'s mess. Unlike most other Navy vessels, *Liberator* had only the one, the old practice of separate messes for the officers and the crew having been abandoned as undesirable, as promoting an artificial class distinction that the experts who designed the ship believed would provoke minor animosities rather than promote harmonious relations.

The spacious mess was situated forward of the bridge and the officers' quarters, in a complex along with the library, the galley, the workout room, and the sick bay. The arrangement was a conscious attempt to have all the living areas in close proximity to give the sub a homey atmosphere. Just forward of the complex lay the crew quarters, followed by the torpedo room and the bow sonar pocket.

Donovan sat at the head of one of the long tables and scanned the anxious faces seated on both sides of him. To his immediate left sat Alex. Beside her was her brother, Peter, the ship's physician and surgeon. Leaner and inclined to be more somber than his sister, Peter Fisher had been spending every spare minute of his time trying to isolate the specific cause of the radiation insanity in the hope of developing a cure. Indicative of the laid-back atmosphere prevailing on *Liberator*, he wore

a white smock and shorts. His hair was tied u
a ponytail.

On Donovan's right sat Communications Officer
Jennings and Chief Engineer Smith.

Apparently no one wanted to be the first to speak.
They all focused on him and waited.

"All right," Donovan began. "We all know what's
happened. I want your input and don't pull any
punches."

Jennings waded right in. "What about Percy and
Burroughs? How long are we going to keep them
waiting? If we go to Blakistone Island to meet this
Captain Rockwood, they could wind up stranded in
Georgia."

"Not to mention the danger to any survivors they
managed to get out of Argyle," Alex said. "They're
bound to run into white-shirts and who knows what
else."

"I'm extremely worried about them too," Donovan
confessed. "Anything else?"

Peter Fisher cleared his throat. "I hate to sound
so callous but I'm intensely curious about Rockwood
and those helicopters. Where do they come from?
What did Rockwood mean about reporting to his
superiors? Who are these superiors?" He paused
and asked almost sheepishly, "Would it really hurt
Percy to wait one more day for us to get there?"

"Pete!" Alex snapped in annoyance.

Donovan came to her brother's defense. "Don't be
upset with him. He's simply doing as I requested
and not holding back. I appreciate his opinion."

"I'm curious too, but I'm not about to abandon
Percy and Burroughs just to satisfy my inquisitive
nature," Alex said, her eyes zinging tiny arrows at
her sibling.

"How do we know we can trust this Rockwood?"
Jennings chimed in, taking the heat off Peter. "Sure,
he passed up a chance to open fire on us. But he could
have been testing us, trying to probe our defenses,

...imply showing us he can be trusted."

"True," Donovan said thoughtfully.

"We might be waltzing into an ambush," Jennings went on. "By noon tomorrow Rockwood could mine the Potomac or set up big guns on the shore."

Peter Fisher snickered. "Aren't you being a bit paranoid? You make it sound as if Rockwood has an entire army and all the ordnance in the world at his disposal."

"How do we know he doesn't?" Jennings retorted.

An uneasy silence descended.

"All the points that have been raised so far are excellent," Donovan said in an effort to keep the ball rolling. "You've hit the nail on the head. No matter what we do, we're taking a big gamble. If we head for Georgia, we blow the opportunity to learn more about another group of survivors. If we go to the island, we leave Percy high and dry. We're damned if we do and damned if we don't."

"I vote we don't go meet Rockwood," Alex declared. "Percy and Burroughs are more important."

"I agree," Jennings said.

Dr. Fisher shrugged. "I guess my vote doesn't matter."

"On the contrary," Donovan said, and glanced at Chief Engineer Smith. "Flazy, what's with you? You haven't said a word."

"Nope," the hefty man replied. "Why bother?"

"I beg your pardon?"

"Why bother, Tom?" Flazy reiterated. "We both know what you have to do, what you're going to do, so anything I say would be beside the point."

Alex looked at the engineer. "Are you a mind reader? Or do you know something we don't?"

Chuckling, Flazy nodded at Donovan. "I can't read minds, but I do know our captain here. He's doing everything he can to pick up the pieces and get the world back on its feet again. And when a crisis arises, when push comes to shove, he always does what's

77

best for the common good, not necessarily wha
would *like* to do."

"So?"

"So we're going to make that appointment at
Blakistone Island and Percy will have to wait."

Everyone gazed at Donovan again.

"Is this true?" Alex inquired stiffly.

"Yes."

"Then why the hell are we sitting here offering
advice if you've already made up your mind?"

"I was hoping you would convince me to change
it."

Alex's nostrils flared. "Convince *me*. Why are we
going to Blakistone Island?"

Donovan rested his elbows on the tabletop. "We
can't pass up this opportunity to establish contact
with other survivors. Think what it would mean
to the colonists on Espiritu to learn they're not
alone, that there is another group trying to salvage
civilization from the ruins. We might be able to
work with these people, to share supplies or conduct trade. Or maybe they'll want to relocate to the
South Pacific. The possibilities are endless."

"And poor Percy?"

Frowning, Donovan stared into her eyes. "John
is a good man. He can take care of himself. I'm
positive he'll stay near the rendezvous site and we
won't have any trouble finding him when we get
there."

"You hope."

"I'm sorry, Alex. Like Flazy said, I have to do
what I think is best for everyone."

"I pray you're not making the biggest mistake of
your life."

"So do I," Donovan said. He stood, moved to an
intercom on the bulkhead, and pressed a black button under the speaker. "Communications?"

"Yes, sir?" came the prompt reply from the man
who had taken Jennings's place.

atch me through to the helm."

In a second the young helmsman's voice sounded loud and clear. "Hooper here."

"This is the captain. Lay in a course for Blakistone Island. As soon as we're clear of the debris in the James River, I want all ahead flank."

Percy slammed on the brakes, sending the Chevelle into a slide, and squinted against the almost painful glare of bright light. For all of ten harrowing seconds he couldn't see the road and feared they would slew off the shoulder and crash into a tree.

Janet continued to scream.

Randy was shouting, "What's going on? What's going on?"

And Burroughs poked his head out his window, peering skyward, shielding his eyes with his hands. "There's something above us! I can't make out what it is."

Percy's vision abruptly cleared, just as the car came to rest at the right-hand edge of the roadway. Leaning over the steering wheel, he gazed upward and was startled to see a flare floating gently toward the ground, the light emanating from an orange canister, of the type formerly used by search-and-rescue teams, that was attached to a small white parachute. He also distinguished the vague outline of an inky craft in the air beyond the flare.

A horn blared and the coupe pulled abreast of the Chevelle.

"What the hell is happening?" Duke shouted. "What's up there?"

"I don't know," Percy responded, wondering if there could be a connection between the craft overhead and the one that had bailed his fat out of the fire earlier. From the way it hovered, the thing must be a helicopter. But who was on it? What did they want?

79

"We're getting out of here!" Duke yelled, and coupe's rear tires squealed as he sped northward.

"Wait!" Percy urged, his cry drowned out by the tires and the roar of the coupe's engine. He wanted to wait, to see if the aircraft descended, since the occupants had to be survivors and possibly friendly. But at the same time he didn't want to become separated from his newfound acquaintances. He hesitated, debating which course of action to take, when a harsh voice, amplified many times over as if by a bullhorn, bellowed from above.

"You there, in the Chevy. Step out with your hands in the air. Leave all weapons inside."

That clinched it. Percy wasn't about to place his life, and the lives of Burroughs and the children, at the mercy of the unknown chopper operators. Whoever was up there might indeed have the best of intentions, but he couldn't afford to give them the benefit of the doubt when there existed even the remotest likelihood they were hostile. He buried the accelerator, the Chevelle responding superbly, and raced after the coupe.

Burroughs, still leaning out the window, declared, "Whatever that is, it's making no move to follow us, sir."

"Keep your eyes on it," Percy instructed, his own glued to the red taillights ahead.

"Mr. Percy," Janet said nervously.

"What is it?"

"That thing might be one of the black helicopters we were told about."

Percy glanced over his right shoulder at the girl. "Who told you? What did they say?"

"Mr. Meyers told us about them first," Janet explained. "You remember. He's the one who helped us after our folks were killed by the zombies."

"Yes, I remember you telling me about him."

"Well, he said that he'd seen these strange black helicopters swoop out of the sky and take people."

ke people?" Percy repeated, mulling the implications while watching the road. The coupe had a
good lead and he'd be hard-pressed to overtake it.

"Yeah. Those were his words. Then, when we were
in Argyle, Mr. Treadwell told us about the time these
bad men in a black helicopter took friends of his off
and no one ever saw them again."

"Why would anyone go around abducting people?"
Burroughs interjected.

"Who knows?" Percy rejoined. "But we're not letting them abduct us."

"Then we'd better haul butt," Burroughs advised.
"That chopper, or whatever it is, is heading this
way."

"I see it!" Randy cried, his face pressed to the rear
window. "Wow! The thing is huge!"

Percy looked in the side mirror but saw nothing
except the flare settling to the asphalt. He stuck
to the center line, every nerve on edge, the skin
between his shoulder blades crawling as if of its
own volition. An intense premonition of impending
danger seized him.

"Here it comes!" Randy shouted.

A immense shadow, darker even than the night
sky, seemed to pass almost directly over the Chevelle
and streaked toward the coupe.

Percy stared heavenward, amazed at the aircraft's
speed, certain it was the same chopper as before.
The 'copter caught up to the coupe in the blink
of an eye and kept pace with the car. Evidently
Duke was aware of it, because the very next
moment the coupe turned sharply to the left,
pulling into a parking lot in front of a long, low
building.

Duke, Maggie, and Yuma burst from their vehicle, leaving the car running and the headlights on,
and made for the entrance, Yuma snapping off several shots along the way.

The helicopter suddenly climbed rapidly.

81

Although tempted to keep on going, Percy w[...]
about to desert the others. They shouldn't have
panicked and sought shelter in the building, where
they could easily be trapped. He glimpsed a large
sign on the left and caught the words BOATS GALORE,
and then he was at the parking lot and turning in.
He braked next to the coupe and shifted into park.
"You three stay here," he ordered. "I'll go get Duke
and his friends out of there."

"Can't we all go?" Randy asked.

"No. Lock the door behind me," Percy said, and
glanced at the seaman. "If something should happen, you get these kids out of here."

"Will do, sir."

Grabbing the Franchi, Percy slid out and dashed
to the double doors fronting the structure. He tried
the knob and found it locked. The headlights partially illuminated the interior and he could see the three
of them just inside. "Open up, Duke!" he yelled.

The blond man complied and motioned for Percy
to enter. "Get in here quick, dude."

"No," Percy replied. "We're sitting ducks if we
stay here. We must keep going." He took a stride
toward their vehicles. "Hurry before that chopper
returns."

"I think we're safer here," Duke objected.

"Me too," Yuma added.

Percy paused, annoyed and feeling exposed standing in the open. He scanned the sky and saw no sign
of the aircraft. "I don't have time to argue. We're
taking off. If you want to come, fine. If not, then stay
here and let whoever is up there nab you." Pivoting,
he hurried for the Chevelle.

"Wait," Duke said, stepping outside. Yuma and
Maggie followed suit, both apprehensively eyeing
the heavens.

Again Percy paused and looked at them.

"What do you mean by they'll nab us?" Duke
inquired.

before Percy could answer a tremendous wind abruptly buffeted them and an ominous black shape descended out of nowhere to hang less than ten yards above their heads. "Run for the cars!" he commanded, and spun to do just that. He managed a single pace, however, when something flashed down and struck him in the left shoulder, lancing his arm with intense pain and causing him to stumble. Stunned, he glanced at his shoulder to find a slender red dart imbedded in his skin. He grabbed for it, intending to tear it loose and continue to the Chevelle, but a surging wave of vertigo engulfed his consciousness in the span of a heartbeat and his mind whirled into a Stygian void.

Donovan sat rigidly in his swivel chair, his eyes roving over the shimmering screen. On his right stood Alex, calm and self-possessed as always. On his left stood Flazy, absently gnawing on an already short fingernail. An almost palpable air of expectancy enveloped the bridge.

"Twenty minutes until noon," Alex commented while consulting her watch. "We'll get there early."

Nodding, Donovan glanced at Helmsman Hooper's back. "Reduce speed to ten knots."

"Ten knots, sir."

"Mr. Jennings, anything on our sensors yet?"

"Negative, Captain. I've conducted a complete sweep of the VHF and UHF bands and picked up nothing. Our passive radar shows no contacts anywhere in the Potomac other than the wrecks, derelicts, and debris shown on Cyclops. Active radar reveals the shore features to be slightly different than those on file."

"Elaborate."

"The Potomac is a quarter of a mile wider at this point than it should be," Jennings said. "The computer projects even more drastic widening farther inland. It looks like a repeat of the Panama Canal situation, Skipper."

Donovan thoughtfully pursed his lips. The Panama Canal had been extensively widened by the

84

rmonuclear devices that took out Panama City and the canal's locks. He guessed that two or more such missiles had been used on Washington, D.C., through which the Potomac flowed, with predictably similar consequences for the waterway. "The channel markers?"

"So far every one has been where it should be. We're smack dab in the center of the inbound shipping channel."

"Current?"

"Minimal. Less than one knot."

"Good," Donovan said. In the Panama Canal they'd contended with a killer current that had threatened to propel the ship straight into oblivion. "Atmospheric readings?"

"There's a light breeze from the northwest, about four knots. Radiation readings at this point are marginally above normal, not enough to pose a danger, but long-range scanning indicates severely elevated levels the closer we get to the capital."

"How elevated are they?"

"It's impossible to be precise since we're still about eighty miles from D.C., or what's left of it, but there's no doubt Washington is as hot as Havana, possibly more so."

Flazy whistled in appreciation.

*Liberator*'s radiation meters had gone off the scale when the ship passed Cuba en route to the Eastern Seaboard. Havana would be uninhabitable for millennia to come.

"Mr. Hooper," Donovan said, "bring us up to periscope depth."

"Rising at ten degrees," the young helmsman responded a moment later.

"How far are we from the island?" Alex inquired.

"Good question," Donovan said, and looked at the communications officer. "Distance to Blakistone?"

"Under two miles and closing."

Leaning forward, Donovan peered at the tiny icon

representing the essentially flat island located on Coltons Point. Northeast of the meeting site were two bays, Saint Clements and Breton, both deep and wide. There was plenty of room for him to take evasive action should the meeting turn out to be an ambush.

"Levelling off," Hooper announced. "We're at periscope depth, Captain."

"Up 'scope."

"Aye, sir."

Donovan stood and stepped to the periscope. He pressed his eyes to the twin lenses, adjusted the light level for the noonday sun, and increased the magnification factor to the maximum setting before focusing on their surroundings.

Here and there small, rippling waves stirred the otherwise placid surface of the Potomac. The sky contained a few white clouds. To the south winged a flock of gulls. The shorelines were over three miles off on either side and several high buildings were visible. Other than the gulls, though, there was no sign of life.

After rotating the periscope three hundred and sixty degrees, Donovan faced dead ahead and studied the outline of Blakistone Island as they cautiously approached it.

"Two targets, Captain," Jennings suddenly declared. "Helicopters ten miles out to the northwest. Their speed is one hundred and sixty miles per hour."

"Evidently they're as eager for this meeting as you are," Alex remarked, regarding her lover critically.

"Try to raise them," Donovan ordered.

Half a minute went by as the communications officer obeyed.

"I have Captain Rockwood at the other end," Jennings declared at last. "Both choppers have cut back to an air speed of eighty."

Quickly crossing to the communications station, Donovan took a proffered microphone and spoke crisply. "This is Donovan. You're very punctual, Captain."

"I have reason to be," came the somewhat tinny reply from the speaker on the console at Jennings's elbow. "It's nice to see you've decided to come. Over."

"How do you want to handle this?" Donovan asked.

"To demonstrate our peaceful intentions, we'll land on the south shore of Blakistone Island and wait for you to join us."

"And what's to prevent more of your choppers from showing up as soon as we surface? How do I know this isn't a trap?"

"You don't," Rockwood admitted, and paused. "And as far as the choppers are concerned, we both know you could reduce the island to cinders the second a blip appears on your radar screen. I'm not suicidal, Thomas."

Despite his reservations, Donovan grinned.

"If it was up to me," Rockwood went on, "I'd demand that you go to the island first and have your sub back off about a mile, but the decision is out of my hands. My commander wants to prove we mean no harm by taking the initiative and putting his life on the line."

"Who is your commander?"

"You'll find out soon enough," Rockwood said. "After we land, I'll walk to the water and wait for you. I won't be armed. Over and out."

Returning the mike, Donovan went to the periscope and scanned the horizon until he saw twin black dots materialize and rapidly grow larger. The helicopters made directly for the island. They were still too far off for him to note much detail. In no time they were hovering over the south shore, then both craft swiftly descended. "They're down," he announced.

87

"Radar isn't picking up any other targe͏̈" Jennings said.

"Mr. Hooper, take us in as close as you can."

"Yes, sir."

"Flazy, get a gun crew ready to take a Walther topside. I'm not taking any chances."

"You bet," the engineer answered, and started to hasten off.

"And get three volunteers to go ashore with me in an inflatable," Donovan added.

"Will you be taking Franchis and sidearms?"

"No. No weapons whatsoever."

"Is that wise?"

"You heard the man. If he's not giving in to his paranoia, neither am I."

Flazy chuckled and departed.

Anxious minutes elapsed as *Liberator* neared Blakistone Island. Donovan peered through the periscope. Jennings stayed glued to his console, studying the monitors that displayed all data relayed by the sensors for any hint of hostile action. Alex gazed intently at Cyclops. Helmsman Hooper skillfully steered the mighty ship toward the south shore. Not a word was spoken by anyone until the very moment Flazy returned with a contingent of crewmen.

"Captain," Hooper declared, "the depth under the keel allows us to draw within seventy yards of the beach. Any closer than that and we risk hitting the bottom."

"Bring us to within one hundred yards, then all stop."

"Yes, sir."

Donovan could see the twin helicopters quite clearly now. The initial impression they conveyed was that of enormous black dragonflies. Each possessed a bubble-shaped cockpit, a narrow, extended fuselage, and short wing-type stabilizers. Everything was black, including the tinted cockpit that

88

ctively screened those within from scrutiny. The otor blades, easily twice the length of the conventional variety, were at rest.

A lone man emerged from the right-hand aircraft and walked the twenty yards to the beach, where he stood with his hands clasped behind his back and stared out over the Potomac, awaiting the sub. He wore a black uniform but no helmet or hat. His hair was blond.

That must be Drew Rockwood, Donovan concluded, trying to distinguish the man's features. Finally he moved back and stated, "Down 'scope."

Flazy came over. "I have those volunteers you wanted and the gun crew is waiting with the Walther at the hatch."

"Take charge of the gun crew as soon as we surface."

"Why me?" Flazy asked in surprise. "I'm no good with a machine gun."

"The crew is. And I want someone I can rely on to stay calm in charge of them," Donovan said, and lowered his voice. "Junior officers have a tendency to be trigger-happy."

"I understand," Flazy said, smirking. "I won't shoot until I see you blown away."

"Has anyone ever told you that you have a pathetic sense of humor?"

"Practically everyone."

"Believe them," Donovan said. He glanced at the communications officer. "Lasers to weapons mode just in case."

"Aye, Captain."

"You'll have the conn while I'm gone, Mr. Jennings. If this is a trap, you will take evasive action and get the hell out of here at the first sign that we've been tricked," Donovan ordered.

"But what about you?"

"I'm expendable. The ship isn't. It's as simple as that."

89

"We won't leave you," Flazy interjected.

"You will if I tell you to," Donovan stressed. He deliberately refrained from looking at Alex, although he could feel her eyes boring into him.

Helmsman Hooper interrupted their conversation with the declaration, "We're approaching the one-hundred-yard mark, Captain. All stop."

"Take us up," Donovan directed, then turned to Flazy. "Get me a transceiver." He paused. "Mr. Jennings, I'll keep the channel open the entire time so you can monitor it. If we're being played for suckers, you'll know the second I do."

Alex made a soft snorting sound. "Which will be a second too late."

Finally Donovan faced her and almost winced at the stark apprehension mirrored in her lovely eyes. "It can't be helped. We're taking all the precautions we can."

Nodding once, Alex swallowed and averted her gaze. "Just take care," she said huskily.

"Hey, you know me."

"It's not you I'm worried about. It's Rockwood."

*Liberator*'s teal-colored titanium-composite hull glistened with moisture when Donovan climbed from the hatch on the topside bridge and trained binoculars on the island. The choppers were still at rest. No one besides the sole man on the beach was in evidence. He moved aft and peered down at the gun crew. The Walther had been mounted, its barrel pointing at the helicopters. Flazy looked up and waved.

Donovan gave the binoculars to the warrant officer manning the topside bridge and quickly climbed down to the foredeck where the three volunteers waited. The inflatable bobbed gently in the water next to the starboard diving plane.

"All set, Skipper," one of the seamen said.

"Let's shove off," Donovan responded. He took the

90

d, climbing into the raft and holding it steady while the others did likewise. The trio manned paddles and the line was hauled in.

On the shore, as immobile as a statue, stood the blond man.

The inflatable moved forward and Donovan glanced at the men doing the rowing. "I want all of you to stay with the raft once we reach the island. If anything happens, try to get back to the ship."

"Will do, sir," replied the same seaman who had spoken before.

Donovan unclipped the transceiver attached to his belt and pressed the transmit button. "This is Red One. Do you copy?"

"Affirmative, Captain," Jennings acknowledged.

"Anything on our sensors yet?"

"The status is the same."

"Okay. I'm locking the channel open," Donovan said, and depressed a circular black button that did just that. He reaffixed the transceiver to his belt, gave the device a pat, and scrutinized the island. Beyond the 'copters stretched a tract of woodland extending a third of a mile from north to south. A flock of starlings flew above the trees. Otherwise, nothing moved.

The man on the beach gave a friendly wave and took a stride closer to the river.

Donovan returned the gesture. He studied the officer as the inflatable narrowed the gap, guessing Rockwood to be in his late thirties, possibly early forties. The man was endowed with a muscular build and a rugged countenance. Various insignia adorned the skintight uniform. There were gold bars on each lapel, a U.S. flag patch on the left shoulder and an unusual red patch depicting a miniature lightning bolt on the right shoulder.

"So it really is you," the man stated when the inflatable was only ten feet off.

Donovan waited until the bow touched the sand

before jumping out and assisting the three crewm[...]
in pulling the inflatable onto the beach. Straightening, he stepped up to the officer and offered his right hand. "Captain Rockwood, I presume?"

"Yes," the blond man confirmed, shaking Donovan's hand and smiling. "And you're Tom Donovan. I recognize you from the photograph in your file."

"My file?"

"Everything will be explained shortly," Rockwood said. "But I'm not the man to do it. The commander wants that honor."

"There you go again," Donovan said. "Who is this guy you keep referring to?"

"Sorry," Rockwood said, chuckling. "I should use his proper title. After all, the commander in chief isn't just my superior. He's also yours."

"The commander in chief?" Donovan repeated, comprehension beginning to dawn, his insight attended by astonishment and budding consternation. It couldn't be! he told himself.

Rockwood laughed. "If you could only see your expression," he said, and nodded at the right-hand helicopter. "I know this will come as a shock to you, but there's someone who is very eager to meet you."

Twisting, Donovan saw a man attired in a blue suit step from the chopper and advance toward them. The newcomer's balding pate, fleshy jowls, and bulldog visage were all too familiar. He'd seen them on many a newscast and many a magazine cover.

"Captain Donovan," Rockwood stated formally, his green eyes twinkling, "allow me the pleasure of introducing the President of the United States."

11

Percy came awake with a start and sat bolt upright, his mind whirling, remembering the mystery aircraft and the red dart that had downed him. He blinked in the glare of bright light and gazed around in bewilderment to find himself seated on a green cot in an otherwise barren cubicle with gray walls and a white tile floor. Someone had stripped off the skinsuit and replaced it with a green gown, the kind typically worn by patients in hospitals. All of his weapons were gone.

He felt stiff and had a mild headache. Pressing his right palm to his forehead, he licked his dry lips and tried to make sense of his predicament. Obviously he'd been taken into custody, but by whom? Why had they done it? What did they want? More to the point, who *were* they?

Percy placed his naked feet on the tile and shivered at the touch of his soles to the cool floor. Scanning all four walls he failed to find a door.

"Don't move!"

The barked command drew Percy's attention to the source, a small speaker situated in an upper corner of the room just below a small video camera, a Minicam mounted on a narrow shelf. A glowing red light under the camera lens indicated the device was in operation.

"You will remain seated, Prisoner number 17123,"

the stern voice commanded. "A guard will be th
shortly."

"Who are you?" Percy responded indignantly.
"What is this place?"

No answer was forthcoming.

Peeved but well aware he could do nothing under
the circumstances, Percy impatiently waited for
someone to appear. Not a minute later he got his
wish.

A hidden panel in the left-hand wall suddenly
hissed wide, revealing a burly man who wore a
strange black uniform and carried a thick metal
rod in his left hand. On the tip of the rod was a
silver metal sphere the size of an orange. "Stand
up," the man instructed gruffly.

"Who are you?" Percy asked, beginning to comply.
"Where am I?"

In two swift strides the man reached the executive officer and extended the rod.

Percy felt the silver sphere touch his shoulder.
Without warning a lightning bolt coursed through
his body, a tremendous surge of voltage that hurled
him from his feet and slammed him against the
wall. His mind still functioned but his body seemed
to be short-circuited as he slumped onto the cot, his
limbs twitching uncontrollably.

"You'll keep your mouth shut unless told to speak,"
the man declared.

Percy's central nervous system was on fire. He
tried to clench a fist, to rise and punch the sadistic
SOB in the face, but couldn't. It was as if his nerves
refused to conduct the mental impulses from his
brain. He lay there quivering helplessly for over
a minute while his body recovered, staring up at
his smirking tormentor. The rod, he deduced, must
be a type of stun gun, a sort of glorified cattle prod
modified for use against humans.

"My name is Lamar," the man stated. "I'm the

n out with darts too? If so, how? There were a zillion questions and no answers. Frustrated, he frowned and went to smack his hand on the cot.

Unexpectedly, the door opened.

Glancing at the entrance in surprise, Percy did a double take at the sight of an attractive blond woman wearing a one-piece yellow outfit styled in the fashion of a military jumpsuit. In her slender hands she held a tray bearing a plate of food and a glass of milk.

"Hello, Prisoner number 17123," the woman said cordially. "I'm Prisoner number 12409."

"Hello," Percy responded, recovering his composure.

"Are you hungry?" she asked, entering.

The mere thought of food made Percy's stomach growl loud enough for her to hear. "I guess I am," he replied.

Grinning, the woman deposited the tray at one end of the cot. "You'll get two meals a day during your stay in the detention ward. The food here isn't half bad. I think you'll like it." She paused, studying him. "It sure as hell beats scavenging for eats."

Percy nodded at the tray. "Thanks," he said, and added the first thing that popped into his head to keep her talking. "Should I address you as sir?"

The blonde laughed. "Not hardly. I'm just a trustee. You call me by my number, the same as with all the other prisoners."

"A trustee?" Percy repeated, then inquired innocently, "What did you do to land such a cushy job?"

A shadow seemed to fall over the blonde's countenance and her lips curled downward. "I'll be back for the tray in thirty minutes," she informed him, and took a pace toward the door.

"Wait," Percy said. "Why are you upset? What did I say?"

Halting, the trustee glanced at the camera. "Noth-

97

ing," she said, her tone strained. "I'm not upset." ̣ͨ
cleared her throat, stepped to the left-hand corner oɪ
the cubicle, and pointed at the wall. "When nature
calls, press this black button."

Percy saw that there indeed was a tiny black button situated at waist height. He'd missed it before.
He watched as she jabbed it with her finger and a
panel moved aside revealing a closet-sized compart-
ment containing a small sink and a toilet.

"As soon as you're done, close the panel," the
woman said, and did so. "If you leave it open, you'll
be disciplined by the guards. And never spend more
than five minutes in there or a guard will be sent
to check on you." She gave him a meaningful look.
"They can get annoyed when that happens."

"Thanks for the tip."

She headed for the entrance again.

"Can't you stay and talk?" Percy bluntly asked.

Pausing in the doorway, she glanced over her
shoulder. "Sorry, Prisoner number 17123, but frat-
ernization between a trustee and other prisoners
while the trustee is on duty is strictly forbidden.
Maybe we'll have a chance to talk after your interrogation and you're allowed free time."

"But—" Percy began in vain, because the next
second the door hissed closed and she was gone.
Disappointed, he picked up the tray and rested it
in his lap. The meal consisted of a bowl of vegetable
soup and a ham-and-cheese sandwich. He tasted
the soup and found the flavor bland. Regardless,
he dug in and had consumed half the bowl when
once again his door opened.

Lamar stood outside. "You son of a bitch."

Dumfounded, Percy froze with the spoon halfway
to his mouth.

His face a livid mask, Lamar came in and the
door shut behind him. "You're not as bright as I
thought you were, asshole."

"What did I do?" Percy queried.

In a rush Lamar was on him. The brutish guard swung the rod like a club and clipped him on the right temple.

Percy fell sideways, pain lancing his head, the tray clattering onto the floor. He lifted his left forearm and warded off a second blow, then attempted to get off the cot.

"Don't move, bastard!" Lamar hissed, extending the business end of the zapper toward Percy's head. "This thing can kill as well as stun."

Percy froze.

"I heard every word you said," Lamar growled. "Prisoners aren't allowed to question trustees. Remember that or the next time I won't go so easy on you."

Although he longed to retaliate, Percy held his surging temper in check. The guard's stark rage perplexed him. In no way did his casual comments to the woman justify the assault. There must be more to it.

"Just remember this warning and you'll be a lot happier," Lamar declared. Wheeling, he pressed a button on his rod and the door opened. With a baleful glare at the executive officer he promptly departed, the panel shutting in his wake.

Percy sat up. His gaze happened to alight on the security camera and he noticed the red light wasn't glowing, which meant the camera had been off during Lamar's attack. Why? Had Lamar turned it off before coming to the cell? He stared at the light until, a minute later, it came on again.

Strange, Percy reflected. What did it all mean? He leaned down and lifted the tray. The rest of the soup and the glass of milk had spilled, forming a large puddle. Thankfully, the sandwich still rested on the plate. He retrieved it and took a hungry bite.

For the better part of ten minutes Percy slowly polished off the ham-and-cheese and tried to put

99

together the pieces of the Site R puzzle. After eac... he used a napkin that had been on the tray and toilet paper from the bathroom to soak up the puddle, then sat on the cot in deep thought.

A half hour after the blonde left, she returned. Her blue eyes flicked from the pile of soggy paper Percy had put on the tray to his face, and her own expression became profoundly sad. Moisture welled in the corners of her eyes. "I take it you're done," she said matter-of-factly.

"Yes, thank you," Percy said, equally formal.

She retrieved the tray from the cot. As she bent down her back was momentarily to the camera and she locked her gaze on his and silently mouthed the words "I'm sorry."

Percy opened his mouth to answer and saw terror etch her countenance. She blinked, her mouth dropped open, and she straightened. He promptly changed his mind, nodding once instead. Her relief was transparent.

"I'll bring you more TP," she offered.

"Thanks again."

"I'll also bring a bar of soap, a washcloth, and a towel. You're required to take good care of them or the guards will discipline you."

"Do tell."

She smiled, turned, and gasped.

Percy stood and faced the doorway, anticipating another run-in with Lamar. But it wasn't the burly guard this time. There were two men in black standing in the corridor, both wearing sidearms, both sporting crewcuts. The thinner of the pair, a man with a hawkish visage, wore glasses and black gloves. He focused on Percy and sternly announced:

"Prisoner number 17123, you will come with us immediately. Resist, and you'll wish you'd never been born."

"Captain Donovan!" the president declared happily in a clipped New England accent, extending his right hand as he approached. "You have no idea how delighted I am to make your acquaintance."

Feeling oddly disoriented, as if he must be dreaming, Donovan absently shook the chief executive's hand. "The pleasure is mine," he mechanically responded, then added almost reluctantly, bothered by a twinge of guilt at questioning the man's status, "Excuse me, sir, but aren't you Harry Murphy, the Speaker of the House?"

Murphy chuckled and lowered his arm. "The *former* Speaker of the House, you mean. As the third official in the line of succession, I automatically assumed the presidency after both the president and the vice-president were killed."

Suddenly Donovan recalled more information about the man now heading the United States. Murphy had served in the House for over twenty years as a representative from the state of Massachusetts. Boston born and bred, and by all accounts an avowed liberal, Murphy had made flashy headlines shortly after the turn of the century by trying to push through Congress a bill authorizing a government-sponsored euthanasia program for terminally ill patients who wanted to end their lives rather than endure continued pain, suffering, and medical costs.

"There's so much we must discuss," the new pre︎
dent was saying. "I want to know all about how you
managed to survive the war, and I'm especially
interested in hearing the details of your encounter
with the *Deutschland*."

"I'll be glad to fill you in, sir," Donovan said,
glancing at the helicopters. "And there's a lot I'd
like to know. Where have you been all this time?
Did any other top officials survive? What are your
plans?"

President Murphy grinned. "All of your questions
will be answered in due course, Captain. For now,
we must return to Site R immediately."

"Site R?"

"Oh. That's right. You probably don't know the
nickname of the facility that currently houses my
administration. But I would imagine you've heard
of Raven Rock, have you not?"

Raven Rock. Yes, Donovan had heard of the place.
It was an immense underground bunker situated
about five miles north of Camp David in the pris-
tine Maryland hills. Formally designated the Alternate National Military Command Center, it could
supposedly withstand a direct hit from a thermo-
nuclear missile. The complex contained accommodations for several thousand people and boasted a
medical clinic, a barbershop, and a spacious dining
hall, not to mention a laundry, a chapel, and even a
racquetball court. Nodding, Donovan asked, "Is that
where you've been staying?"

"Yes. I was one of the fortunate few who got out
of Washington within minutes of receiving word
about the attack on the carrier in the Sea of Japan.
Had I not taken it on myself to be flown to Raven
Rock, I would have perished with the majority of
my colleagues."

Taken it on himself? The statement sparked a
disturbing train of thought that Donovan promptly suppressed. Since he hardly knew the man, he

uld give him the benefit of the doubt.

Captain Rockwood cleared his throat. "Excuse me, sir, but what about the other Dragonflies? Do you want them to take their positions?"

"By all means," the president answered.

The officer reached behind his back and produced a black transceiver into which he barked orders. "Lieutenant Spencer, this is Rockwood. Move Beta Flight into position."

"Beta Flight?" Donovan said quizzically. "What's going on?"

The answer came a moment later when three more black helicopters rose from behind the woods and swooped toward the river.

"What is this?" Donovan demanded, grabbing his own transceiver, wondering if the meeting might not be a trap after all.

"You can relax, Captain," President Murphy said. "The three Dragonflies have been assigned to patrol this stretch of the river and safeguard *Liberator* until I decide where she will be permanently based."

"Until *you* decide?"

"Why, certainly. I *am* commander in chief of the U.S. military and *Liberator is* a Navy vessel, is she not?"

Donovan nodded, stunned by the turn of events, a swarm of butterflies fluttering in his stomach. The president had the legal authority to take command of *Liberator* should he so desire. As an officer in the U.S. military, Donovan knew he must submit to whatever decision the chief executive made. But he couldn't help experiencing a degree of resentment at having his command of the ship treated in so cavalier a fashion. He glanced at *Liberator* and suddenly thought of something. Whipping the transceiver to his mouth, he pressed the proper button and said, "Mr. Jennings, this is Donovan. Everything is under control. Repeat. Everything is under control. The new choppers don't pos\_ threat. Do you copy?"

"Aye, Captain," came Jennings's rather curt reply. "We've been monitoring the conversation on the open channel. Standing by for *your* further orders."

Out of the corner of his eye Donovan saw President Murphy's bulldog countenance harden. He quickly stated, "That will be all for now. I'm flying with the president to Raven Rock. I'll be in touch as soon as I can."

"Yes, sir. Take care. Over."

Rather sheepishly Donovan reattached the transceiver to his belt.

"You have a loyal crew, Captain," President Murphy commented in a brittle tone.

"They're the best, sir. They'd follow me to the gates of hell if need be."

"Loyalty is commendable," Murphy said, "provided it is properly placed." He abruptly smiled and clapped his hands. "Well, now. Why don't we get started for Raven Rock? We have so much to talk about."

"Yes, sir," Donovan said, and looked at the volunteers who had accompanied him to the beach. "Take the inflatable back to the sub and stay there until I come back."

"Aye, Skipper," one of the seamen said.

President Murphy opened his mouth as if to say something, then apparently changed his mind and continued toward the helicopters.

Keeping pace on the chief executive's right, Donovan pointed at the black choppers and remarked, "I take it these helicopters are called Dragonflies?"

Captain Rockwood answered from the president's left side. "That they are, Thomas. I have twenty-four of these babies at my disposal. They're the aviation equivalent of your sub, light-years ahead of their time. They're faster and more powerful than

104

chopper ever built. With them I could—"

"That's enough, Captain Rockwood," President Murphy interrupted. "I'm sure Captain Donovan is interested in more than your precious Dragonflies. If he wants, General Hawke will fill him in at Raven Rock."

"General Simon Hawke?" Donovan inquired in surprise. He'd met the four-star general once at a social function. Hawke had been one of the top brass at the Pentagon, a staunch conservative renowned for his annual battles with Congress over military appropriations. If Congress cut one cent, the good general had cried foul.

"Yes. He's my second-in-command."

The disclosure shocked Donovan. He recalled reading once that Murphy and Hawke practically hated each other. What strange combination of circumstances had conspired to make political bedfellows of such a disparate pair? "Haven't you selected a vice-president yet?" he thought to ask.

President Murphy snorted. "Why do I need a vice-president? The office always was superfluous."

Donovan said nothing further until they came to the Dragonflies. He was troubled by Murphy's attitude. The man appeared too arrogant for his tastes, but maybe he was judging the new president prematurely. Murphy must be under supreme strain, what with trying to get the devastated country back on its feet. Such unbearable stress would make any person edgy and temperamental.

On the cockpit door was the same emblem as on Rockwood's uniform, a bright red circle slashed by a lightning bolt down the center.

"I've never seen this before," Donovan commented, indicating the symbol with a nod.

"As well you shouldn't have," President Murphy said. He touched the emblem almost affectionately. "It stands for COG."

"The Continuity of Government program?"

"Yes. Certain aspects of the program were high
classified, including the existence of an elite military unit composed of the cream of the crop from
the Army, Air Force, Marines, and the Navy. The
COG Corps, it's called. Only a few top administration and congressional officials with a clear need to
know were aware of the corps's existence."

Captain Rockwood nodded. "I was recruited for
the corps from the Air Force, then sent to a top-
secret training facility operated by the CIA. After
I completed the special program I was assigned to
Raven Rock Security. Other corps members were
assigned to Mount Weather, Sherman Valley, Butte
One, and other underground survival centers."

Donovan shook his head in amazement. The
shocks just kept coming. To think that the U.S. government had formed a clandestine military force and
concealed it from the American people! What other
secret projects had the government been involved
in but never let anyone know?

The president grinned. "I can tell just by looking
at you, Captain Donovan, that all of this comes as
a bit of a surprise."

"A bit."

"Well, as the colloquialism goes, you haven't seen
anything yet."

"I can hardly wait," Donovan said dryly.

"That's the spirit," President Murphy stated, and
glanced at Rockwood.

The officer quickly opened the cockpit door and
stood aside so they could enter first.

"After you, Captain," the president said.

"Thank you, sir," Donovan responded politely, and
climbed in.

While it wasn't apparent from outside, the cockpit
was quite spacious, with seating for six in addition to the pilot, who sat in the very nose. Three
men in black already occupied the foremost of two
cushioned benches. They faced straight ahead,

omatic weapons cradled in their laps.

Donovan moved to the rear bench and slid over against the far side. He gazed out the cockpit bubble at the Potomac River, observing his men row the inflatable toward *Liberator*. An intense longing to be with them filled his soul and he suppressed the feeling. He knew he should be happy at learning that the U.S. government was still intact, but instead he felt disturbed. His attention drifted to the three Dragonflies assigned to guard the sub. They were flying in formation back and forth across the river.

The president sat down beside Donovan, then Captain Rockwood vaulted into the aircraft and closed the cockpit door.

"All set, sir," the officer stated.

"Excellent," Murphy said, and looked at the pilot. "Site R, James, and don't spare the juice."

Donovan smiled mechanically at the joke.

Leaning forward, Captain Rockwood looked at him and advised, "You'd better fasten yourself in, Thomas. Flying in one of these is like taking a carnival ride."

"I'll vouch for that," President Murphy said good-naturedly.

Watching the pilot flick toggles and press buttons, Donovan secured his web seat belt. No sooner had he done so than the Dragonfly abruptly rose straight up, attaining an altitude of one hundred feet in three seconds. The force of the sharp ascent pushed his body back against the seat.

"What did I tell you?" Rockwood said. "Get set. Here comes the fun part." He glanced at the pilot. "Lieutenant Chaney, show our guest what this bird can do."

"Yes, sir."

From his previous contacts with the mystery choppers Donovan knew they could fly at incredible speeds. The first Dragonfly he'd sighted had

been clocked at one hundred and ninety-two mi̱
an hour. But that knowledge did little to prepare
him for the astounding acceleration that next took
place. One instant the Dragonfly was hovering
above Blakistone Island; the next the helicopter
was streaking northward like a jet, the ground
below a virtual blur.

Rockwood laughed lightly. "Flying a Dragonfly
is the ultimate flying experience. Its top speed is
two hundred and ten and it's as maneuverable as
a hummingbird."

"I'm impressed," Donovan said, trying in vain to
note landmarks below.

"An LJT-12 aerial navigation and guidance computer assists the pilot," Rockwood boasted. "It's
housed in the nose and protected by heavy armor
plating."

"So far we've mainly used the Dragonflies for
patrol and reconnaissance missions," President
Murphy disclosed. "But their role will expand once
we take the offensive."

Donovan's head snapped around. "You're planning to attack someone, sir?"

"Of course, Captain. You don't think for a minute
that we're going to let the Germans off the hook so
easily, do you? This war isn't over until the fat lady
sings."

President Murphy intended to continue the war!
Donovan sagged in his seat, flabbergasted. What
in the world had he gotten himself into? Even
more importantly, how could he get himself out?
Profoundly perturbed, he swung his head to the
left and looked out the cockpit to prevent anyone
from seeing his expression. Then the president said
something that agitated him even more.

"General Hawke and I will fill you in once we
arrive at Raven Rock," Murphy promised, and patted Donovan's right knee. "Your new home."

Percy was ushered down a long, cool corridor by
the two men in black. Neither bothered to draw a
weapon although the hawkish man kept his right
hand on the butt of his pistol. Overhead fluores-
cent lights afforded illumination. Both walls were
metallic, the floor white tile. He passed dozens of
cubicles just like his own and distinguished by black
numbers situated above the sliding doors. If not for
the numbers he would never have known the doors
were there, so perfectly were their edges blended
into the walls proper.

The guards spoke only twice, when the hawkish
man gave directions. Once they took a right at a
junction, the next time a left.

They passed just two other people en route to
their destination. The first was Lamar, who glared
at Percy. The second was another woman wearing
the yellow garb of a trustee. She rather fearfully
averted her eyes.

Percy wished he wore pants instead of the green
gown. With every stride he took he felt a draft on his
private parts. It gave him a feeling of vulnerability
and prompted him to speculate on whether compelling the prisoners to wear such attire was a
deliberate psychological ploy to intimidate them.

"Hold up," the hawkish man suddenly announced
as they drew abreast of yet another sliding door, this

one bearing the designation INTERROGATION ʀ painted in large block letters above it.

Obediently stopping, Percy waited while the other guy stepped to the wall and pressed one of those tiny black buttons. The door hissed wide to reveal a ten-by-twelve room containing a small metal table ringed by four metal chairs.

"Take a seat," the hawkish man directed.

Percy moved around the table to sit facing the door. His escorts entered and the door closed again.

"I am Lieutenant Stewart," the hawkish man disclosed, finally taking his hand from the pistol. He nodded at his companion, who walked behind Percy. "This is Sergeant Maxwell."

"You aren't by any chance related to Lamar, are you?" Percy quipped, grinning, and instantly regretted his flippancy. Something struck him from the rear on the right temple, filling him with agony. He doubled over, pressing his right palm to his head, grimacing, and waiting for the pain to subside.

"You will not speak unless spoken to," Lieutenant Stewart snapped.

Percy twisted and saw Sergeant Maxwell holding a short steel baton in his right hand. He let his eyes express his appreciation of the blow.

"Give us any trouble and the good sergeant will repeat the discipline," Stewart warned. He sat down across from the executive officer and calmly folded his hands on the tabletop. "Are you composed enough to begin?"

Nodding, Percy straightened, unprepared for the second blow, which hit his left temple. He cried out and clutched his throbbing head, stars exploding in front of his eyes.

"You will answer verbally when questioned," Lieutenant Stewart stated coldly. "Failure to comply will result in additional discipline."

Percy suppressed an urge to tell the son of a bitch

110

, he could do with his discipline.

Now let's begin, shall we?" Stewart went on clinically. "Ordinarily we wait at least a week before interrogating prisoners. The extended incarceration gives us a psychological edge." He paused. "But in your case, Prisoner number 17123, we've made an exception. Would you like to know why?"

"Yes," Percy answered harshly, then flinched in expectation of another blow because he'd neglected to add a servile "sir." But Maxwell didn't strike him.

"You merit special consideration because you intrigue us," Stewart said. "Most of the survivors brought to the detention ward are your typical ignorant, malnourished, dirty scavenger types who have been roaming aimlessly since the war. Predictably they resent being retrieved and resist reclamation."

Percy tried a tactic that had worked with Lamar. He tentatively raised his right hand.

"Yes?"

"Am I permitted to ask questions?"

Lieutenant Stewart pondered the request for a bit before replying. "Very well. I'll allow you to ask whatever you want." His tone became flinty. "But I warn you now that I expect your full cooperation or else. Understood?"

Looking over his shoulder at Maxwell, Percy answered, "Loud and clear, Lieutenant."

"Good." Stewart leaned back and studied the prisoner. "I'll satisfy some of your curiosity right now by telling you that you're at Raven Rock, an underground bunker the size of Baltimore located in Maryland. Site R, we call it."

Percy stared at the man's black uniform, focusing on a strange red patch bearing a lightning bolt. "You're part of a government military unit."

"Very perceptive. Yes, I'm part of the corps."

"The Marine Corps?"

Both Stewart and Maxwell laughed.

"No, not those wimps," the lieutenant stated. "I'm referring to the COG Corps, the military arm of the postwar administration."

"Never heard of it."

"I would imagine there's a lot you've never heard of," Stewart said. "Which brings up another point. Our retrieval team was quite surprised to—"

"Retrieval team?" Percy interrupted.

Stewart pursed his lips in annoyance. "Yes. We have airborne units constantly scouring the countryside for survivors, who are picked up and brought to Raven Rock."

"Whether they want to come or not."

"Our retrieval teams must resort to tranquilizer darts because most citizens resist being brought here. They resent being drafted."

"Drafted?"

"Yes. The president has imposed a mandatory draft of all able-bodied citizens, all men, women, and children who haven't contracted the radiation sickness or some other disease. If we're to get America back on her feet we must restock our labor pool."

Restock? The term made it sound like the corps was collecting cattle, not people. Percy didn't let his repugnance show. "I thought the president was killed when the Germans nuked the carrier in the Sea of Japan."

The lieutenant exchanged a glance with the sergeant.

"He was," Stewart confirmed. "Harry Murphy, the former Speaker of the House, has succeeded to the post. He's doing a damn fine job, too. The draft is just one of the measures he's imposed. The entire country is now under martial law and will probably stay so for the next century."

Percy thought the man must be joking but Stewart didn't crack a smile.

the rate we're going," the officer went on, we'll meet our quota of drafted citizens within three months and then we can begin phase two of Operation Rebuild."

"How does all of this affect me?"

"I'm glad you asked," Stewart said. He reached into a shirt pocket and produced a set of dog tags on a silver chain. "Recognize these?"

Percy didn't need to read the name, rank, serial number, and blood type engraved on the tags to know whose they were. Obviously, they were his. He nodded and extended his right hand, palm up. "I'd like them back, if you don't mind."

"No can do, Executive Officer John Percy," Lieutenant Stewart said a tad sarcastically. "Prisoners aren't permitted any personal possessions while in the detention ward."

"Since you've known my identity all along, why did you incarcerate me?"

"Your rank and naval status mean nothing to us. As far as we're concerned, the Navy, Army, Air Force, and Marines no longer exist. The sole military arm of the United States is now the corps," Stewart said. "And until we get truthful answers to a few puzzling questions, you'll stay confined." He replaced the dog tags in his pocket.

"I'm willing to cooperate," Percy stated honestly. He'd go along with them for the time being in the hope of being released from the cell.

"That's refreshing to hear," Stewart said. "Most survivors give us a hard time during their interrogation. They must be persuaded to obey."

As Percy sat there staring at the officer, at Stewart's crisp black uniform and haughty expression, an image popped unbidden into his mind attended by an appropriate descriptive phrase: storm trooper. The smug lieutenant reminded him of stories he'd read about the sadistic Nazis who lorded it over their fellow Germans in the days prior

113

to World War Two. He shook his head to dispe[l] troubling image. Stewart, after all, was a Unite[d] States military officer, not a Nazi.

"Is something wrong?" the lieutenant asked.

"No."

"Good. Then let's proceed. And bear this in mind. We have a complete file on you, everything from your kindergarten days to your midshipman years at Annapolis and your subsequent naval career. We know, for instance, that your first grade teacher, a Mrs. Roswell, had several meetings with your parents to discuss your aggressive attitude. It seems you were always getting into fights," Stewart related.

Percy listened in amazement. How could they possibly know that?

"We also know that you were rated third in your class at the Naval Academy. You received straight A's in the courses that appealed to you the most, namely naval science, military tactics, and mathematics. You were on the varsity football team the year Navy clobbered Army forty-one to twelve. You were also on the boxing squad and had a record of nineteen wins and no losses."

"How—?" Percy began, but the lieutenant continued speaking.

"Your psychological profile rates you as a first-rate officer but you made the Navy brass a bit nervous because of your passion for war games. In every combat maneuver in which you participated, you won. One of the reasons they assigned you to *Liberator* was in the hope Captain Donovan would have a positive, dampening influence on your belligerent nature," Stewart said, smirking. "Am I on target so far?"

"Where did you get all this information?"

"It's stored in your computer file. Back in the eighties, when the Defense Mobilization Planning Systems Agency was formed to implement COG rams, the administration authorized the creation of a central computer registry on every American citizen. Tax records, financial dealings, medical histories, criminal records, you name it, it went into the files. Of course, the records are more extensive on prominent officials and high-ranking members of the military. Background checks were conducted on hundreds of thousands who rated special attention, such as yourself."

"Why me?"

"Because you were assigned as second-in-command on the most advanced submarine ever constructed. Naturally, COG would want to know all there was to know about you."

"Naturally."

Stewart chuckled. "There's no need to be offended. We have even more information on Donovan. COG is very thorough."

"You *are* talking about the Continuity of Government program?"

"What else?"

Absently staring at the floor, Percy felt the gravity of the shocking revelations begin to sink in. To think that the United States government had accumulated massive secret files on every citizen! Such a hideous tampering with the fundamental privacy of law-abiding Americans violated every constitutional safeguard of individual freedom.

"You seem to be taking this rather hard," Stewart remarked.

Percy looked at him. "I never would have imagined such a program existed. Why was it done?"

"I should think the answer would be apparent. The basic rationale behind our war planning, you might remember, was that the government must survive any conflict at all costs. No matter how devastated the country became, war was viewed as eventually winnable if the government continued to exist. Why else were all the underground installa-

115

tions constructed specifically for our nation's
ers?"

"And the average person on the street?"

"All the Joe Blows and Susie Sunshines hardly
matter in the world scheme of things, now do they?
The government never bothered building survival
shelters for them. Why waste the funds?"

The awful truth of the man's words brought a
horrifying insight to Percy. He remembered that
the U.S. government had indeed occasionally given
lip service to civilian defense preparedness but had
never done a damn thing to ensure that a sizeable
segment of the population would survive a global
Armageddon despite repeated warnings from civilian experts. Not even after the hard-liners returned
to power in the Soviet Union had anything been
done. He abruptly felt very queasy.

"Are you all right? You look sick."

"I'm fine."

"The doctors examined you when you were brought
in and gave you a clean bill of health. You shouldn't
be ill."

"I'm fine," Percy reiterated.

"Well, let's get down to cases. We want to know
where *Liberator* has been since the war. What has
Donovan been up to? What were you doing dressed
in a blacksuit and armed to the gills near Saint
Andrew Sound? Were you on a clandestine mission?
Tell us everything that has happened to you. Hold
nothing back. Remember, you owe us your life."

"I do?"

"Sure. One of our 'copter crews bailed your fat
out of the fire when you were surrounded by white-
shirts, remember? They sized you up through their
night-scope and decided to lend a hand, then reported the sighting to headquarters. The general himself made the decision to bring you in."

"Lucky me."

Stewart nodded. "So let's get under way. Start at

eginning and give us every detail."

Percy looked the lieutenant in the eyes and with full realization of the impending consequences stated angrily, "Go to hell." He never even saw the blow to his right temple that knocked him to the floor.

The Dragonfly decelerated and banked toward a particularly prominent Maryland hill covered with verdant woods except at the top and the bottom. On the crest lay a four-acre parking lot half filled with vehicles and a spacious landing pad on which rested four other helicopters. On the east side of the hill, extending for fifty yards along its base, reared a two-story concrete wall. In the center of the wall a great access tunnel large enough to accommodate three tractor-trailers driving side by side served as the sole entrance to the underground facility known as Raven Rock. The entire hill was enclosed in a ten-foot-high chain-link fence capped with triple strands of sharp barbed wire. Guards wearing black COG uniforms patrolled the perimeter and there were two squads stationed at the closed front gate.

Donovan took all of this in as the Dragonfly descended toward the landing area. He glimpsed a few white-shirts in the trees to the west. "Do the zombies give you much trouble, Mr. President?"

"Not near as much as they used to," Murphy replied. "Site R was intentionally built at a remote location but the white-shirts eventually found it. About two weeks after the war there were hundreds outside the fence every day trying their damnedest to break in. Since we keep the fence electrified with

118

thousand volts, they didn't stand a prayer. our guards expended thousands of rounds of ammunition in disposing of them."

"And now?"

"Now they rarely mount a full-scale attack, although there are always a couple of dozen prowling around the fence. They've learned the hard way."

"I didn't think the white-shirts possessed the ability to reason, sir."

"Oh, they don't think in the same way you and I do, but they do have a rudimentary intelligence, even if it is single-minded. The C-210 has that effect, you know."

Donovan had no idea what the president was referring to and went to inquire about it when the Dragonfly alighted on the asphalt at the top of the hill.

"At last!" Murphy declared.

Captain Rockwood reached for the door, then glanced at Lieutenant Chaney. "Have this bird refueled and ready to lift off in an hour."

"Yes, sir," the pilot responded.

Rockwood opened the door and moved aside so the chief executive and Donovan could get off first.

"I dislike being away from here for even a minute," Murphy commented as he stretched. "It's the only place I feel truly secure."

A note of genuine apprehension in the president's tone caused Donovan to surreptitiously study the man's face. He detected a flicker of fear in the man's eyes as Murphy gazed at the forest beyond the fence.

"Where the hell is that Jeep?" the chief executive snapped.

Turning toward the parking lot, Donovan saw that most of the vehicles were caked with dust. Apparently no one had used them in months and he mentioned as much.

"Where would the owners go?" Murphy aske[d] torically. "Outside the fence there's certain d[e]⸺ At least here everyone is safe."

The growl of an engine drew Donovan's eyes to the southern edge of the hill where a black Jeep had just driven over the rim and was following a narrow road toward them.

Captain Rockwood stepped to the president's side. "Do you want me to escort you below, sir?"

"Of course," Murphy answered testily. "I must be protected at all times." He craned his neck to peer overhead. "We're probably under surveillance at this very moment."

"Surveillance?" Donovan repeated skeptically.

"Yes. Didn't you know, Captain, that the Germans put a spy satellite in orbit about a year before they started the war?"

"No, I didn't."

Murphy looked at him. "I must remember to upgrade your security clearance status now that you're serving as one of my personal advisors."

"I am?"

"Certainly. As commander of the corps's nuclear sub, you're entitled to special privileges."

The corps's nuclear sub? A chill rippled along Donovan's spine at the thought of having his ship mustered into the COG military arm. What the hell was he going to do? He felt as if he were being torn in half emotionally. On the one hand was his oath of allegiance to the United States and his obligation to follow the orders of the chief executive implicitly, and on the other was his responsibility to the colonists on Espiritu and his commitment to his crew. He owed it to his men to let them have a say in *Liberator*'s fate. His conscience wrestled with his sense of duty and attained a temporary stalemate.

In no time the Jeep arrived and swung around to brake in front of the president.

about time," Murphy said sternly to the driver, who blanched.

"Sorry, sir," the man in black said. "I was in the john when the announcement came over the speaker that your choppers were landing."

"So what's more important?" Murphy demanded. "Me or your bodily functions?"

The driver faced straight ahead. "It won't happen again, sir."

"See that it doesn't. And pass the word to the other drivers."

"Yes, sir."

Donovan climbed in the back beside the chief executive. The more he learned about Harry Murphy, the less he liked. Murphy wasn't merely arrogant; he was downright dictatorial.

Rockwood sat down in the front passenger seat. "Okay, Sergeant. Let's go."

The Jeep sped toward the south rim.

Out of the blue, President Murphy posed a profoundly distressing question. "How soon can you have your crew ready to be brought to Site R for orientation, Captain Donovan?"

Dumfounded, Donovan gazed out his window, stalling, his mind in a whirl. Technically, legally, he should comply without question, but he balked at the notion of putting his people at Murphy's mercy.

"Well?" the chief executive prompted impatiently.

"Is orientation necessary, sir?" Donovan inquired.

"Most definitely," Murphy declared. "The corps orientation program will inspire them to do their utmost and remain steadfastly devoted to their government. Why, even the Marines who were selected for the COG Corps were required to take the orientation program. You know how patriotic Marines traditionally were, but they had to be even more so in support of COG."

"How long does this orientation take?"

"Oh, about four weeks all told," Murphy disclose[d] "By the time your people complete the course I can guarantee they'll be new men."

The president's inflection gave Donovan pause. Who ever heard of Marines needing to be *more* patriotic? To him the orientation sounded like a subtle form of brainwashing.

"We could take your crew in shifts," Murphy proposed. "Say, half at a time. That way you can be out to sea within two months."

"What will our destination be?"

"I'll let General Hawke give you the details," President Murphy said. "We stayed up late last night discussing our war strategy. I can't begin to tell you how excited we were when Captain Rockwood reported the details of his encounter with you and the meeting he'd set up on the island." He paused. "We were so worried that it would turn out to be a trick, that the *Deutschland* would show up, not *Liberator*."

"The *Deutschland* is resting at the bottom of the Pacific."

"And good riddance. Without their supersub, the Germans will easily be defeated."

Donovan lapsed into a contemplative silence as the Jeep wound down the hill and turned toward the access tunnel. All of the guards snapped to attention as it passed.

The chief executive glanced nervously out the front gate. Dozens of yards beyond the perimeter, loitering in small groups at the edge of the forest, were a few dozen white-shirts. "God, I hate them," he muttered.

Into the mammoth tunnel they went, streaking down the center line. Rows of lights on both walls and overhead bathed the roadway in a harsh glare. There were guard posts positioned every hundred yards, with two men standing on small platforms

sed into either wall. Also on every platform
s a large machine gun mounted on a tripod.

President Murphy pointed to the top of the right-
hand wall. "No one can get in or out of Site R
undetected," he boasted.

Donovan looked and saw a security camera
mounted on metal brackets. Whoever had designed the place hadn't missed a trick. The security
arrangements were outstanding.

"Raven Rock is impervious to attack," Murphy
bragged. "The outer shell of the structure consists
of ten feet of solid concrete. It's rated to withstand
a direct hit."

"So was Mount Weather, sir," Donovan noted.
"Have you heard from them?"

Murphy's features clouded. "No, I'm sorry to say.
We've tried to contact every other bunker without
success. The relay satellite could be out of commission, but I fear the worst. I did send several
Dragonflies to Mount Weather since it's the closest,
and all they found was a mountain of rubble to
mark the spot where the entrance had been."

The Jeep took a gradual curve to the left, moving
at forty miles an hour. Ahead appeared a checkpoint, a barrier gate similar to the type used at
railroad crossings, manned by a dozen troopers in
black. The officer in charge saw the Jeep approaching and barked orders that resulted in the barrier's
being raised before the Jeep reached it. All the
troopers stiffened at attention until the Jeep had
gone on by.

"How far down does this go?" Donovan inquired.

"Half a mile."

Down and down they went, passing two more
checkpoints along the way, the tunnel changing
directions several times before they ultimately arrived at an immense parking facility where dozens
of Jeeps, convoy trucks, tanks, half-tracks, and a
few sedans were already parked, the tanks and

half-tracks in separate rows off on the left si

The driver made for the right side of the parkⁿ
area and stopped next to one of a series of double
doors lining the wall. Painted in bright red letters
on the outer panels was a warning:

RESTRICTED AREA
ONLY THOSE WITH PRESIDENTIAL ACCESS
OR MAJESTIC CLEARANCES MAY
PROCEED BEYOND THIS POINT.
PRESENT IDENTIFICATION AT CHECKPOINT.

A dozen corps personnel stood at attention just
outside the doors. At their head stood a tall man
with short black hair and dark eyes whose black
uniform bore four rows of ribbons. His angular face
broke into a grin as he stepped forward.

"Mr. President, I see our prayers have been
answered."

Murphy hopped out and warmly shook the man's
hand. "Yes, indeed, Simon. Beyond our wildest
imaginings."

Sliding out, Donovan self-consciously smoothed
his shirt and stood at attention himself.

"General Hawke," President Murphy said, ges-
turing at Donovan. "I'd like you to meet the man
who is going to give us victory on a silver platter."

"Captain Donovan," the general declared, stepping forward. "This is a momentous occasion."

Saluting smartly, Donovan mustered a smile and
said, "It is?"

"Most definitely, Captain," Hawke asserted happily. "Thanks to you and your ship we now have
the means of carrying the war home to Germany."

Murphy cleared his throat. "Let's discuss this in
private, shall we?" He walked to the double doors
and barged on through.

"After you," General Hawke said to Donovan,
motioning with his right arm.

Resigned to going along with them until he had

pportunity to present his views on *Liberator*'s
are activities, Donovan squared his shoulders
and walked through the double doors into a wide,
brightly lit corridor. He trailed after the chief executive, who had already covered ten feet and seemed
in a hurry to get somewhere.

Behind a mahogany desk on the right stood a
lieutenant. Five armed corps members stood along
each wall. The weapons they carried slung over their
shoulders were unlike any Donovan had ever seen.
Shaped much like machine guns, these unusual
models appeared to be composed of sleek black
plastic and contained no magazines. The stocks
were much larger than normal and at the end of
each barrel was a fist-sized smooth sphere.

General Hawke, walking at Donovan's side, observed the objects of his attention and chuckled.
"Rather unique, aren't they, Tom?" He paused. "I
can call you Tom, can't I? After studying your file
all last night and this morning, I feel as if I know
you personally."

"What file would that be, General?"

"Call me Simon. Why, that would be the COG file.
I'll bet you weren't aware that COG maintained a
file on every American citizen?"

"No, sir. I wasn't."

"Yep. Those superconducting computers made it
all possible. No limits to their storage capacity and
they function instantaneously. I believe you have
the Cray-9 on *Liberator*?"

"Yes, sir."

"Well, we have the Cray-10 here, a prototype that
can beat the Cray-9 hands down. It's at least twice
as fast."

"And those strange guns?"

"M-49s. Sonic disrupters. They use sound waves
to destroy any target they're aimed at. One shot
would blow your chest apart."

125

"I've never heard of them," Donovan sa[id] amazement, gazing over his shoulder at one of [the] M-49s.

"The disrupters were developed a year before the war. Classified 'eyes only.'"

Donovan faced front, his lips compressing. There seemed to be no end to the surprises, no end to the secrets. The corps. The Dragonflies. The COG files. M-49s. He couldn't help but wonder with a degree of trepidation: What next?

Charlie awakened to the sound of someone furiously pounding on the door of his hut. He promptly sat up, trying to collect his wits, and yelled, "I'll be right there."

The pounding continued unabated.

"What the hell could have happened?" Charlie muttered, wondering if the dogs might have attacked another colonist. By all rights the canines were supposed to be trapped up on the cliff. Four guards were now guarding the trail at all times to prevent the pack from descending. He slid from his rumpled bed, found his clothes lying on the floor, and quickly got dressed.

Whoever was out there seemed determined to break down the door.

"I'm coming!" Charlie bellowed. The loaded Franchi was in the room, propped against the corner. He retrieved it and hastened from his bedroom. In four long strides he reached the front door and pulled it wide open.

Just outside, his arm uplifted to pound yet again, stood one of the men from Charlie's gunnery detail, one of the four who'd stayed behind with him when *Liberator* departed.

"About time, sir," Seaman Richards commented dryly. A lean, sinewy man who sported a neatly trimmed mustache and a clipped beard, he was best shot on the sub next to Charlie. "I about wore out my hand."

"What's going on?" Charlie demanded. "Are we under attack by hostile natives? Have the dogs found another way down?"

"Nothing like that," Richards said, shifting so he could point to where the three other members of the gunnery detail stood. Seamen Wayne, Kent, and Parker were standing with their heads tilted back, staring skyward in astonishment.

Charlie scanned the village and saw every other colonist in sight doing the same thing. "What the—?" he began, and looked up himself. Not knowing what to expect, he was totally dumbfounded at what he saw.

Circling lazily a hundred feet above the ground directly over the village was a hang glider, or at least a contraption that strongly resembled such a craft. V-shaped, with long green canvas wings that flapped slightly as it soared, the glider hardly appeared sturdy enough to support the massive pilot: Baltimore Jack.

"What is that lunatic up to now?" Seaman Richards asked.

Before Charlie could answer, Jack spied him and waved.

"Yo, Charlie!" the big ex-wrestler called out, and dipped the nose of the glider to swoop low over the huts. "Meet me at the cliff!" he shouted.

"What are—" Charlie tried to reply, but the hang glider arced upward, banked sharply, and headed toward the volcano.

Richards snickered. "You never know what that guy is going to do next, do you?"

Well aware of Jack's intent and peeved at the crewman's sarcastic attitude, Charlie snapped, "Follow me." He made for the jungle, motioning for the other seamen to join him.

already the hang glider was hundreds of yards off and gaining altitude rapidly.

Wayne, Kent, and Parker caught up with Charlie and Richards. Strung out in a line with Charlie in the lead, they entered the lush vegetation and angled to the northwest.

"Do you know what's going on, sir?" Seaman Wayne, the youngest member of the detail, inquired. A robust youth with curly black hair that spilled out from under his white cap, Wayne possessed the questionable distinction of being known as *Liberator*'s heartthrob. The rumor mill had it that no less than three daughters of different colonists were warm for his handsome form.

"Baltimore Jack is going to try and get that glider above the cliff so he can check on the dogs," Charlie answered while running.

"Is he crazy?" Richards commented. "The air currents aren't strong enough to lift a lug like him. A stunt like that could get him killed."

The factual assertion prompted Charlie to increase his pace. Where in the world had Jack obtained the glider? He reflected, his gaze straying to the ungainly aircraft still trying to climb higher. He estimated Jack was almost five hundred feet up, which meant the ex-wrestler needed to gain over five hundred more, preferably six, in order to sail safely above the escarpment.

Charlie threaded through the underbrush as fast as he could, battering limbs aside, plowing across stretches of waist-high vegetation, and creating quite a racket in the process. Spooked birds and parrots screeched or squawked and flew off for quieter climes. Monkeys chattered angrily at the intrusion into their verdant domain.

He repeatedly lost sight of the glider as he passed under tall trees. In a large clearing he paused for a second to get his bearings and saw Baltimore Jack had attained a height of eight hundred feet and

was spiraling ever higher. Taking a deep br̶e̶a̶t̶h̶
he plunged onward, sweat caking his skin.

None of the others bothered to speak. They forged
steadily ahead without complaint, spurred by Charlie's sense of urgency. All of them were lacerated by
the sharp tips of limbs on their hands and faces.
A cloud of tiny, buzzing insects engulfed them at
one point and stayed with them for almost fifty
yards, compelling the men to swat wildly as they
ran. Parker stumbled and would have fallen if Kent
hadn't been there to catch him.

Charlie was breathing hard by the time they
drew within a hundred yards of the precipice. He
gazed up.

Still spiraling in wide circles, but not quite at
the thousand-foot elevation yet, Jack was gamely
climbing higher.

Don't try it! Charlie wanted to shout, but he
knew he'd be wasting his time. He raced toward
the base of the cliff and spied the four colonists on
guard duty, two men and two women, all carrying
rifles. They were gawking heavenward in transparent amazement.

With great relief Charlie burst from the jungle at
last and slowed. He had to tilt his head way back to
see the hang glider, which was almost level with the
top of the escarpment.

"Charlie!" one of the women called out. "What's
going on?"

Seaman Richards answered her. "That lunatic
nature boy is trying to commit suicide."

While normally Charlie enjoyed the wisecracking
Richards's company and considered the man a good
friend, he felt a flush of anger at hearing Jack
belittled again and spun to glare at the surprised
crewman. "That'll be enough out of you."

"Sorry, Charlie," Richards blurted, extending his
hands palms outward. "I didn't mean to tick you off.
I know you and the lug are sort of tight."

130

e's a friend," Charlie said testily, "and a good man. I won't let anyone insult him in my presence. Understood?"

Just as Richards went to respond one of the women vented a short scream.

"Look! His glider!"

Charlie whirled and stared upward, horrified to find that a small section of the canvas covering the left-hand wing appeared to have been torn loose from the very tip of the frame and was flapping vigorously.

"Jesus!" a colonist exclaimed.

"He'll come down now," Richards predicted.

But the giant apparently had no intention of landing yet. Jack twisted his head and looked at the fluttering canvas, assessing the damage, then faced front and continued to gain height.

Charlie held his breath as the hang glider slowly rose above the cliff. Jack gazed down at them and waved.

"That guy sure has guts," Seaman Wayne commented.

The torn wing flapping even harder, the giant banked the aircraft and swept out of sight over the rim far above.

"What if he crashes?" asked a woman. "We'll never be able to get up there and help him."

"He won't," Charlie said, his voice strained with tension, his left hand gripping the Franchi so hard his knuckles were white, his right clenched so tightly that his fingernails bit into his palm. He scanned the rim, waiting for the hang glider to reappear.

Each second that elapsed was like an eternity.

"You know," Richards said thoughtfully, studying the nearly sheer wall of rock, "I bet we could climb up there if we really had to. We could rig up some climbing gear like the mountain climbers use."

Suddenly the hang glider streaked into view. The wing had torn even more and there appeared to be a gap between the canvas and the frame.

Charlie expelled a long sigh of relief. He smiled, thinking the giant would now descend. In disbelief he watched Jack perform a tight loop and zip over the cliff again.

"What the hell is he doing?" Seaman Kent muttered.

From above came a chorus of faint howls.

"Think the dogs have seen him?" a woman wondered.

Mopping a forearm across his brow, Charlie moved backwards a few yards, trying to glimpse more of the air space above the escarpment, hoping to catch a glimpse of Jack. All he saw, though, were several gulls to the east.

"Will someone kindly explain to me why that man is risking his life and limb?" inquired a male colonist.

"Beats the hell out of me," Seaman Richards said.

"He's doing it for the dogs," Charlie stated.

"The dogs?"

Charlie glanced at him. "Yeah. He's concerned for their welfare. He's checking out the top of the cliff to determine how many are in the pack and whether they have any food or water up there."

"How do you know?" the colonist inquired. "Did you give him permission to pull a stunt like this?"

"No," Charlie said. "But I know him, know the way he thinks."

"Oh, God!" one of the women wailed.

Stiffening, Charlie looked up, his heart seeming to stop at seeing the hang glider spiraling downward out of control. The tear in the damaged wing had widened to where half the canvas flapped violently.

"He's going to crash!"

Accenting the cry, the glider abruptly pitched almost vertical, still spiraling, then righted itself. The giant appeared to be straining mightily to retain

132

a semblance of control but the aircraft dipped
five hundred feet in twice as many seconds.

"Please," Charlie said softly. "Please."

The hang glider went into a sharp dive, the
nose nearly straight down, gaining speed swiftly,
streaking toward the hard earth below. Baltimore
Jack was valiantly striving to pull the nose up,
his massive muscles bulging, his face flushed red.
Resisting his every effort, the glider plummeted to
three hundred feet.

Two hundred.

One hundred.

A woman screamed.

Belatedly, Charlie realized a fact that all of them
should be concerned about: the hang glider was diving directly toward the spot where they stood.

Percy dimly became aware of his own body. His consciousness struggled up out of nothingness and was immediately assaulted by agonizing waves of pain that buffeted his brain mercilessly. Slowly his memory returned. He recalled being interrogated, recalled refusing to divulge any details about *Liberator*'s activities since the war. And he'd paid for his obstinacy.

Sergeant Maxwell had gone to work on him with that wicked steel baton, inflicting torment that had racked Percy to the core of his being. Lieutenant Stewart had laughed throughout the torture session, and when Percy had curled up into a fetal position to protect himself, Stewart had walked over and delivered several brutal kicks to Percy's side.

Yes, sir, Percy reflected. He owed those sons of bitches, and one way or the other he was going to make them pay. Suddenly he realized he wasn't alone. Hands touched his cheeks and he opened his eyes in alarm and sat up, expecting to find himself in the interrogation room. Instead, squatting beside his cot in his cell, was a vision of loveliness.

"Don't bother moving," Prisoner number 12409 advised. "I can only stay a second. Lamar and the other guards are taking a coffee break. There's no one in the monitor room at the moment but one em could return at any time." She glanced nervously up at the camera.

Percy had to force his sluggish lips to move, and when he spoke the sounds he uttered resembled the croaking of a frog. "What's your name?"

"My name isn't important. Listen, I heard Lamar saying that you're going to be interrogated again and again until you tell them whatever it is they want to know. You won't be getting any food or water, either."

"Your name?" Percy persisted.

"What the hell does it matter?" she responded, and looked at the camera again. "Okay. I'm Gloria Harrison. Satisfied?" She lowered her voice. "I smuggled in some fruit, two apples and an orange. They're wrapped in tissue paper and hidden behind the john. At least you'll get a little to eat. Just remember to flush the seeds and peels down the toilet."

"Thank you," Percy said, looking into her eyes. "But why are you doing this for me?"

"Because, like practically every other prisoner here, I hate these corps scum." Gloria stood and backed toward the entrance. "I'm sorry, but I must go. I've stayed too long as it is." She bestowed a compassionate gaze on him and swiftly departed.

Staring at the now-closed door, Percy grinned. He had an ally, someone who might be able to help him escape from the detention ward. From the information he'd gleaned so far, all the prisoners must hate their overseers. Perhaps he could use that hatred to his advantage.

His first concern had to be the next interrogation session. Make that torture session. There were limits to his endurance, and sooner or later the sadistic scum would succeed in wearing him down. He didn't quite understand why the corps was so interested in learning everything there was to know

135

about *Liberator*'s activities since the war, b
rather die than tell them.

Then, too, the longer the sessions continued, the
weaker he'd become. At a certain point trying to
escape would be out of the question. He had to do
something soon. But what?

Sitting up, grunting from the agony in his limbs,
Percy glared at the camera just in case one of the
guards was watching him, then stiffly arose and
shuffled to the bathroom. He walked to the sink and
splashed water on his face. There was no mirror,
probably because the guards didn't want the prisoners to have access to glass that could be broken
and used as makeshift weapons. He didn't need a
mirror, anyway, to gauge the extent of the damage
done to his poor throbbing body.

The bathroom was the only part of the cell that
couldn't be monitored by the camera. He flipped a
finger in the direction of the door and sat down on
the throne. Earlier Gloria had warned him not to
spend more than five minutes in there or a guard
would come, so he began ticking off the seconds
in his mind. One thousand-one. One thousand-two.
One thousand-three.

He found the fruit and took out an apple. Replacing the others, he began eating heartily, wolfing
the apple down, well aware a guard could arrive
at any instant. In no time he'd polished it off and
was tempted to eat the seeds also. Instead, he sent
the core swirling down the commode.

Percy moved to his cot and sank down in relief.
He wondered what time it was and how long he'd
been in the detention ward. By this time Donovan
must have arrived at the rendezvous site and was
either still waiting for him or had headed for home.

Home? Yes, Espiritu now deserved that distinction. He smiled at the thought. If someone had
told him a week before the war that he'd one day
regard an exotic South Seas island as his place of

...nce, he would have laughed in their face.

... idea struck him. Was that the reason the corps wanted to know about *Liberator*'s activities, to discover if there were pockets of survivors elsewhere? From the remarks Lieutenant Stewart had made, he knew the corps's lousy retrieval teams were picking up every healthy survivor they could find. What would happen if the corps learned about Espiritu? Surely the island was too far off for them to touch, but he couldn't be certain. The COG military arm might have capabilities he didn't even suspect.

The hissing of the door interrupted his contemplation.

Lieutenant Stewart and Sergeant Maxwell were framed in the doorway. They entered. Both were smirking.

"Awake so soon?" the officer commented. "You're tougher than I gave you credit for."

Percy fluttered his eyelids, pretending to be on the verge of passing out. "Screw you," he muttered.

Stewart nodded at the sergeant, who came forward and stood at the head of the cot.

"That smart mouth of yours will get you executed at the rate you're going, asshole," Maxwell said, and cuffed Percy on the mouth just hard enough to make the executive officer's lips sting terribly.

"Get the fool on his feet," Stewart directed.

Maxwell slipped his hands under Percy's shoulders from behind and lifted Percy into a sitting posture.

Feigning weakness, Percy stayed limp while the noncom raised him from the cot. He let his body sag, his legs dragging, as the stocky man swung him around to face the officer.

"He's in no shape for another session, sir," Sergeant Maxwell said.

"We shall see," Lieutenant Stewart replied, and stepped in front of the prisoner.

Percy almost grinned in triumph. He had ▓
right where he wanted them. And if Lamar and ▓
other guards were still shooting the bull instead of
watching the monitors, he could pull it off. Even if
there was someone in the monitor room, if he moved
fast enough he might still able to swing it. If. If. If.
There was only one way to find out.

"Are you ready for more fun and games?" Stewart
asked. He snickered and jabbed the fingers of his
right hand into Percy's ribs. "We wouldn't want
you to become bored." With a light laugh he started
to turn.

Now! Percy told himself, and uncoiled in a blur
of motion. He drove his right foot into Stewart's left
knee and heard a loud snap even as he straightened
and swept both hands up and over his shoulders to
grip the sergeant by the chin and the hair. Surging
downward, bending at the waist, he flipped the
noncom over his right shoulder, causing Maxwell
to crash onto Lieutenant Stewart, who was stooped
over and clasping the shattered knee.

The force of the throw combined with Maxwell's
weight to bring both corps members smashing onto
the floor.

Percy promptly waded in. Maxwell was trying to
stand. Percy delivered a combination of punches, a
quick right, left, and right again, to the tip of the
sergeant's chin and the noncom crumpled.

Lieutenant Stewart cursed and clawed at his holster.

Spinning, Percy took particular delight in raining
a flurry of punches on the officer's face. He battered
Stewart flat, his powerful blows reducing Stewart's
mouth to a pulpy mass.

Both men in black were momentarily stunned.

Percy swiftly appropriated their auto pistols, Colt
.45s in the popular officers' model, and with a gun
in each hand dashed to the entrance and peeked out
the doorway.

.enty-five feet to the right, Gloria Harrison was
. emerging from another cell. There was no one
else in sight.

Darting out, his naked feet making hardly any
sound on the white tile, Percy sprinted up behind
her.

Gloria heard him at the last instant and turned,
her eyes becoming the size of half-dollars. "What—!"
she blurted.

"Quick. Where's the monitor room?" Percy inquired urgently while glancing right and left.

To her credit, Gloria recovered her composure
immediately. "This way," she said, and led him fifteen yards along the corridor to a conventional door.
She halted shy of the jamb and motioned for Percy
to pass her.

Gripping the Colts firmly, Percy eased to the
edge of the door and peered through the glass pane
comprising the upper half.

Within lay a control room consisting of dozens of
monitors mounted on all four walls and consoles
underneath. Seated in one of three swivel chairs
was Lamar, his eyes glued to an open magazine
that depicted a young woman posing seductively
in her birthday suit on the cover. Behind and above
him was the monitor linked to the camera in Percy's
cell. Stewart and Maxwell were still on the floor but
the sergeant was stirring. A few feet past Lamar, in
the corner, stood another conventional door slightly ajar.

Percy had to move rapidly. If Lamar so much as
glanced over his shoulder, he'd see the interrogators
and stab an alarm button. "Open the door for me,"
he whispered to Gloria.

Nodding, she took hold of the knob, gave him
a reassuring smile that also conveyed a hint of
affection, and threw the door wide while leaping
out of the way.

In two bounds Percy was in the control room with

both Colts pointing at the man in black.

Startled, Lamar looked up and froze, except his mouth, which worked soundlessly. The girlie magazine fell from his hands.

"Make one move and you're dead," Percy said softly, glancing at that ajar door. What lay beyond it? The break room? Were the other guards still in there having coffee? In confirmation came the faint drone of voices and gruff laughter.

Lamar looked to his left at a console. Resting on top was his zapper.

"Try it," Percy whispered, striding forward with both pistols trained on the guard's head. "*Please* try it."

Staring up into those twin barrels of imminent death, Lamar gulped and shook his head.

"You're a smart Neanderthal," Percy told him. "Now lie on the floor with your arms outspread. Make sure your nose touches the tile."

Demonstrating remarkable alacrity, Lamar obeyed.

Percy heard the corridor door close and glanced back to see Gloria grinning at him. "How much do you charge for baby-sitting?" he asked, nodding at the prone guard.

She came over, her expression transforming to spiteful stone as she regarded Lamar. "I'll do it for free if I get to beat his brains out."

About to hand her a Colt, Percy's gaze strayed to the zapper. He wagged a barrel at the rod. "Do you know how to use that thing?"

Gloria nodded. "He's bragged about it enough," she answered, and carefully stepped around the burly man to retrieve the device.

"Can it really kill someone?" Percy inquired.

"Sure can," Gloria said, indicating a red button. "One press of this and it discharges all of its voltage at once. Fries whoever it's touching."

Lamar budges, fry his ass," Percy directed while moving to the other door.

"Gladly."

Halting near the narrow gap between the door and the jamb, Percy heard more laughter. He peeked through the opening and saw a narrow hallway six feet in length leading into a break room. He glimpsed a long table ringed by metal chairs. Mounted on the far wall was a television screen. There were three guards seated at the table, all conversing while watching the tube, their backs toward him. Lying on the table near each man was a zapper.

"These walls are soundproofed," Gloria mentioned. "Don't worry if you have to shoot."

"Thanks," Percy whispered. He eased the door wide with his right toe, then sped down the hall into the room, levelling both .45s. "Gentlemen," he barked.

The trio of men in black eight feet away turned, each registering a different degree of surprise.

"On the floor," Percy ordered.

Instead, the beefiest of the guards snatched up his zapper and rashly charged. His action served as the catalyst for the others to do likewise.

Evidently they intuitively felt that at least one of them would reach him. Their courage was commendable, but Percy couldn't let any of them get close enough to use those deadly rods. He had a sole recourse, and even as the beefy guard thrust a zapper at him Percy fired, the pistol booming and bucking in his right hand.

The slug bored into the beefy guard's forehead and burst out the rear of his cranium. He dropped where he stood.

Percy squeezed off two more shots. At such short range he couldn't miss, and the other two guards joined their companion on the cool tile. He watched one of them convulse, then pivoted and ran toward

the control room. Several feet from it a sicke
stench assailed his nostrils, an odor so disgusting
he felt his stomach heave. He halted in the doorway, shocked at the sight before him.

Gloria Harrison was on her knees near Lamar.
Her arms sagged at her sides, the zapper dangling
from her limp right hand. Tears filled her eyes.

Still prone on the floor, his body now contorted
like a pretzel, his face a hideous mask, his skin
scorched, his clothing smoldering with tiny flames
dotting his charred back, was Lamar. His thick
tongue protruded from between his fried, blackened
lips. His eyes were locked in disbelief, staring off
into empty space.

Percy went over to her and squatted. "Are you all
right?"

A single nod signified her reply.

"Did he try to take the zapper away?"

Gloria coughed and shook her head.

"Did he budge?"

"No," Gloria said, the word barely audible.

"Then why—" Percy began, and stopped when she
looked at him, her face conveying the torment of a
soul in profound turmoil.

"He . . ." Gloria began, then dabbed at her eyes
and sniffed. "He had his way with me. Told me if I
didn't cooperate he'd make my stay in the detention
ward sheer hell." She paused. "He used the zapper
on me a few times to prove his point."

Percy stared at the grisly corpse. The son of a
bitch had gotten exactly what he deserved. He
decided his earlier comparison had been right on
target: these corps types *were* the equivalent of
storm troopers, as vile as any rabid fascists who
ever existed. Whether simple guards like Lamar or
interrogators like Stewart and Maxwell, the corps
members exhibited a single-minded fanaticism in
their devotion to their duty, which in itself was

....inable enough, but they also indulged in the most callous brutality with no apparent remorse or regret whatsoever. It was as if the members of the COG Corps didn't possess a shred of moral or ethical fiber. They were more like programmed automatons than human beings.

He shook his head and glanced up at the monitors, alarmed to see Sergeant Maxwell blinking his eyes and sluggishly moving his hands. The noncom would be on his feet in another minute. "Stay here," he directed, rising and making for the entrance. He paused to look at her. "If you can pull yourself together, do you think you can find the switches that will open every damn cell in the detention ward?"

Gloria nodded and wiped her sleeve across her nose. "No problem," she said softly. "All of us trustees were given the run of the ward. I've been in here a dozen times and watched Lamar or one of the other guards operating the consoles."

"Good. I'll be right back. Then we'll go from cell to cell and organize the prisoners," Percy said, reaching for the doorknob.

"What do you have in mind?"

"We're going to try and escape from Raven Rock."

"But we're half a mile under the earth's surface and we'd have to fight Site R Security every foot of the way up," Gloria noted forlornly. "No one has ever escaped from Site R before."

"Then we'll be the first or die trying."

143

"He's going to crash on top of us!" one of the female colonists shouted as the plunging hang glider dived straight at them.

Everyone scattered.

Charlie ran toward the forest a dozen feet, then halted to watch his friend. He saw Baltimore Jack straining to his utmost, but even the giant's prodigious might seemed unequal to the critical occasion.

Suddenly the glider's nose swept upward and the aircraft shot out of its dive at a ninety-degree angle, levelling off at a height of fifty feet above the ground and streaking toward the jungle.

"He did it!" Charlie cried happily. His elation, however, proved short-lived.

The hang glider was still moving at an incredible speed, far too fast for Jack to slow it down before the glider reached the verdant wall of vegetation. The ex-wrestler tried to lift the nose higher, to clear the tops of the trees, but his efforts were in vain. Like a huge V-shaped arrow the fragile makeshift aircraft speared into the jungle with a resounding crash, shearing off limbs twenty feet up, plowing a path through the foliage while simultaneously shattering into pieces, disintegrating under the impact. Only the right wing was still partially intact when the craft lost momentum entirely and tumbled to the earth.

ck!" Charlie cried, and raced in the glider's
wake, frantically shoving undergrowth aside, taking the straightest course despite the obstacles. In
his mind's eye he envisioned his friend lying broken
and bloody.

The others were hard on his heels.

"Jack!" Charlie repeated, passing a broken por-
tion of the aircraft. He covered over twenty yards,
anxiously scouring the ground and the trees, looking
right and left. "Can you hear me? Where are you?"

"Not so loud there, little buddy. I've got a hell of a
headache."

The casual reply stopped Charlie in midstride. He
swung to his left, amazed to behold the giant lying
on his back in the center of a patch of waist-high
grass, several busted branches lying underneath
him. "Jack!"

"Please, little buddy," Baltimore Jack said, pressing a palm to his bruised forehead and sitting up.
His clothes were torn in a dozen places, his skin lacerated terribly. He expelled a breath and glanced up
at the overhanging boughs. "I must be the luckiest
dude alive."

Charlie ran to the ex-wrestler's side and squatted.
"How do you feel? Is anything broken? How the hell
did you live through that?"

A wry grin curled Jack's mouth. "Whoa there, guy.
Slow down. One question at a time if you don't
mind."

The gunnery detail and the four colonists ringed
the colossus, all of them staring at him in disbelief.

"Sorry," Charlie said, chuckling. "You had me worried there for a minute."

"Had *you* worried?" Baltimore Jack said, and
snorted. "Brother, I thought for sure I was going
to buy the farm. When that baby finally pulled up
I wanted to whoop for joy until I saw I was heading
for the trees."

"How badly are you hurt?"

145

The ex-wrestler gingerly moved both arms legs. "Everything appears to be intact. There are no broken bones as near as I can tell." He touched his brow. "My head took the brunt of the crash, which is a good thing for me. It's hard to damage solid marble."

Charlie laughed in heartfelt relief, forgot himself, and gave Jack a slap on the back.

Wincing, Jack arced his spine. "Be careful, dude. I may be in one piece but I'm sore all over."

"Thank God you're alive," Charlie said, then thought of all the anxiety the giant had put him through. "Now what the hell was the big idea of pulling a stunt like that without checking with me first? And where in the world did you get a hang glider?"

"I built it," Jack responded while inspecting a wicked cut on his right forearm.

"Say what?"

"After we parted company yesterday I snuck out of the village and went back to my house. Spent the rest of the afternoon and all of last night working on the thing," Jack said, and snickered. "Didn't do a bad job, if I do say so myself."

"Hold the phone, sport. Where did you get the parts to build a hang glider? And where did you learn to fly one?"

"I flew them all the time when I was younger. Got pretty good at it, too. As for the parts, all it took was some canvas from a tent I didn't have any use for and extra sections of metal piping I had on hand in case of plumbing problems."

"I'll be damned."

"You've got to remember that I figured on being largely self-sufficient out here. My basement is crammed with stuff I might need if something should break down. I've even got my own shop with decent welding equipment."

"But how did you get that contraption airborne?"

ample. I just hauled it up the volcano a few hundred feet and jumped."

Charlie glanced at the others, who burst into hearty laughter, then at the giant. "What if the glider had fallen apart? You could have been killed."

Baltimore Jack shrugged. "I wanted to check on the dogs and that was the only way to do it. Everything was fine until the lousy canvas started to rip." He rubbed his head. "I'm still not sure how I wound up on my back. I remember getting knocked off the glider by a big limb and then sort of bouncing from branch to branch until I hit Mother Earth. Whew. Talk about a rough landing."

"Thank God you're alive," Charlie said, and peered up through the trees at the rim of the cliff. "So tell me. After all you went through, what did you find out about our canine friends?"

"I saw sixteen adult dogs and eight younger ones that were less than a year old, I'd guess. Two of the adults were females with small pups born less than a month ago from the looks of them."

Charlie thoughtfully scratched his chin. "That's more than we figured."

"Yep. There are several caves up on top and the dogs are living in them. And they have plenty of water because there's a small spring near the caves."

"What about food?"

The giant grinned. "That's where we have them. There's very little vegetation and no sign of other wildlife. If they want to eat, they must come down here."

"And sooner or later they'll become hungry enough to do just that no matter how many guards we post," Charlie concluded, and stood. "Okay. You've learned what we needed to know." He glanced at Richards. "Go to the village and call a general meeting of the colonists. We're going to present the situation and organize digging details."

147

"Digging details, sir?"

Charlie nodded. "We know the dogs will have to use that trail down from the crest. It's the only way to descend. So we'll dig a wide pit around it, a few yards out from the base of the cliff. Then we'll cover the pit with thin limbs and add a layer of leaves, grass, and weeds. We can also make nets from whatever spare rope we can find." He chuckled. "We'll be just like big game hunters. With any luck, we can capture every damn dog."

"And then what?" Richards asked. "Do we blow them away?"

Charlie looked at Baltimore Jack. "No. I don't think killing them is necessary. Someone once told me that we should treat all living things with the respect they deserve, so we'll give these dogs the benefit of the doubt and try to domesticate them."

"Is that possible?" Seaman Parker inquired.

"I don't know," Charlie said with a shrug. "I remember reading that one of the ways professional trainers would gain the trust of the dogs they handled is by feeding them. Once a dog becomes dependent on a person for food and water, the dog will be that person's friend for life. I guess the way to a dog's heart is through its stomach."

"Sounds a lot like most men I know," one of the women commented.

Only the other woman bothered to laugh.

Seaman Richards gazed at the cliff. "If you ask me, sir, we're going to a hell of a lot of trouble for a bunch of lousy, flea-ridden mutts that—"

Suddenly a certain irate giant loomed over the crewman, his brawny hands on his broad hips, his flinty eyes narrowed slits.

Richards stared into those eyes, blinked, and finished his statement. "That are well worth the effort. So what if we bust our humps? Saving the poor little doggies is more important."

148

timore Jack beamed and draped a huge arm
across Richards's shoulders. "You know, I used to
think you didn't have the brains of a gnat. Now I'm
having second thoughts. Keep this up and you and
I will get to be good buddies."

"Lucky me."

Alex stood on the topside bridge and stared
apprehensively at the south shore of Blakistone
Island. Movement to her right drew her attention to one of the sleek black Dragonflies slowly circling *Liberator*. She frowned, then pivoted
and spotted the other two hovering off to the
west.

"Do they give you the creeps, too?"

She turned and nodded at Chief Engineer Smith,
who leaned against the railing a few feet away.
"They sure do."

"I can't make up my mind whether they're actually protecting us or making certain we don't go anywhere," Flazy remarked somberly.

Nodding, Alex gazed at the island again. "We
should have heard from Tom by now. Why hasn't
he contacted us?"

"Maybe he's simply been too busy. I would imagine the president has been briefing him, filling him
in on the situation. They must have a lot to discuss.
I wouldn't start worrying yet."

"Are you serious? I started worrying the minute
he left the sub."

Flazy grinned, then became solemn. "If it's any
consolation, all of us feel the same way. Here you'd
think that everyone would be overjoyed at estab-
lishing contact with the government, but none of us
are. The comment President Murphy made about
basing *Liberator* at a site of his choosing has upset
everybody." He paused. "I think we've all grown to
like our life on Espiritu over the past few months.
None of us want to leave our island paradise."

149

"But Tom doesn't have any choice, right? I [know] if the president orders him to move everyone back to the States, Tom must comply. Isn't that true?"

A shadow seemed to descend over Flazy's fleshy features. "Given that Tom took an oath of allegiance to the United States and legally must do whatever the commander in chief requires, yes, it's true." He stared at one of the Dragonflies and frowned. "Once, right after the war, I would have agreed wholeheartedly with the president. I would have leaped at the chance to find a suitable base in the States. Now, I'm not so sure."

"I *know* I don't like it," Alex remarked. "The idea of living in one of those underground bunkers gives me goose bumps. And if we live anywhere on the surface we'll have to contend with the constant threat of the white-shirts, not to mention all the radioactive and bacteriological toxins contaminating the environment. It would be sheer hell."

"Maybe we're being premature," Flazy said, although his tone lacked conviction. "Maybe it won't be as bad as we suspect."

Suddenly the bridge speaker crackled to life and Communications Officer Jennings spoke urgently. "Alex? Flazy? Are you still up there?"

Alex was the closest so she responded. "We're here, Dave. What's up?"

"I need both of you down here on the double," Jennings declared. "We have major trouble."

"What is it?"

"Just get down here."

Clicking off, Alex glanced at Flazy, who shrugged, and they both hastened below and onto the bridge. All appeared to be in order; the crewmen were manning their posts, some engaged in idle conversation. As they approached the communications console, though, Jennings swung his chair around to face them, anxiety etching his features.

"What's up?" Alex asked.

ennings gazed past them to ensure none of the crewmen were listening, then motioned for them to step right up to his chair. "I just received a call from Raven Rock," he informed them.

The news made Alex brighten. "From Tom?"

"No," Jennings answered. "From General Simon Hawke. He's instructed me to prepare to receive a boarding detail."

"What?" Flazy blurted.

"That's right," Jennings confirmed. "A fifteen-man detail is on its way even as we speak."

"But why?" Alex asked.

"The general told me the detail is going to go through the ship with a fine-tooth comb, conducting systems checks, auditing our stores, and generally rating our readiness for a sea tour."

"Did Tom give his consent?" Alex inquired.

"I don't know," Jennings said. "When I requested to speak with the captain, the good general told me that he's in a meeting with the president and can't be disturbed at the moment. Hawke promised to have Donovan contact us soon."

"But by then this detail could be on board," Alex noted.

"Exactly."

Flazy wrung his hands together. "The skipper left you in charge, Dave. What are you going to do?"

Angrily pounding his right fist into his left palm, Jennings glowered and snapped, "I wish to hell I knew."

18

Seated in a metal folding chair in an enormous briefing room at Raven Rock, Donovan listened to the chief executive discourse at length about the war and its aftermath. Beside him on the right sat Captain Drew Rockwood, who had been informally appointed his escort for the day by President Murphy. General Hawke had excused himself and departed a while ago and had yet to return.

Ten feet away at the head of the chamber, standing beside a huge map of the United States that covered the entire wall, Murphy extended a pointer he held in his right hand and tapped New York City. "The Big Apple was the first city hit," he disclosed. "Broadway, Times Square, the Statue of Liberty, they were all incinerated in the blink of an eye."

"I know. I've been there, sir," Donovan commented.

Murphy paused, as if thrown off his verbal stride by the interruption. "That's right. One of our Dragonfly patrols spotted *Liberator* en route to New York. Why did you go there, by the way?"

"To rescue survivors."

"Were you successful?"

"Yes, sir. We picked up two men who had contacted us by shortwave, their wives, and six iren. All of them are currently on the sub," Donovan mentioned.

President Murphy beamed. "Excellent. The more survivors we retrieve, the sooner we'll have America back on her feet again."

He paused. "How many survivors have you rescued since the war?"

Donovan hesitated. So far he'd refrained from informing the President about Espiritu and the colonists making a new home there. Although by all rights he should let Murphy know, he felt oddly uneasy about doing so. He could just see the president ordering him to bring every last colonist back to the States, a duty he didn't view as justified. So to avoid a potential dispute, he'd kept silent. Now, continuing the subterfuge, he fibbed. "We've saved about two dozen, all told."

"And they're all on *Liberator*?"

"Yes, sir," Donovan lied again.

"Good. Then you can turn them over to us. I'll arrange for Dragonflies to pick them up," Murphy said, casting a meaningful glance at Captain Rockwood.

"Whenever you want, sir," Rockwood stated.

Hoping to change the subject, Donovan nodded at the immense map and asked, "Do you have any idea how many survivors there are in the U.S.?"

"Our computers can't provide an exact figure," Murphy answered, "but the projections run into the hundreds of thousands. Of course, there would be many more if it weren't for the damn white-shirts. But no one could have foreseen the effects of the C-210."

There was that designation again. "What is C-210?" Donovan asked.

"A chemical warfare agent we employed during the conflict," President Murphy said. "We launched over two hundred missiles bearing chemical warheads, all containing the new C-210."

153

The United States had used chemical weap.
Donovan couldn't believe he'd heard correctly. "...
I thought the use of chemical weapons had been
banned by the accord reached in Geneva after the
war with Iraq?"

"My good captain, you are so politically naive,"
Murphy said with a chuckle. "Of course the U.S.
signed the United Nations accord. So did every other country who belonged to the world body. But neither Russia nor the U.S. destroyed all of its stockpiles."

"What does this C-210 have to do with the white-
shirts, sir?"

"Everything," the president replied, frowning.
"You see, upon impact a C-210 missile would
disperse a gigantic cloud of the chemical agent.
The wind would then carry this cloud over the
countryside, and everyone who breathed the toxin
died instantly. These clouds were designed to be
extremely long-lived. Barring contact with rain,
any given cloud of C-210 possessed a cohesive life
expectancy of a week and a half."

"That long?" Donovan exclaimed in amazement.

"Yes. We were trying to maximize the kill factor. Unfortunately, as our scientists have now confirmed, the longevity worked against us."

"How so?"

"I'm no scientist," the chief executive said, "but I
can give you a fair idea of what occurred. I've been
briefed several times on the cause of the disease that
produces the white-shirts." He paused, collecting his
thoughts. "You see, the problem started when all the
radioactive particles floating in the air came into
contact with the C-210. The radioactivity actually
mutated the primary chemical agent in the C-210,
resulting in a virus unlike any ever seen before.
Oh, there was a similar precedent, of sorts. We
know that the radioactivity unleashed during the
Central American War in the Andes mutated the

154

virus and resulted in a particularly deadly neurotropic virus that was quickly cured. This time around we're not so fortunate, though. Our best minds have been unable to find a means of coping with the new mutant strain."

Donovan nodded absently, appalled by the oversight. Why hadn't the scientists who created C-210 thought to study the effects of radiation on the agent since they must have been aware that nuclear and chemical-tipped missiles would be used simultaneously?

"We'll get the white-shirts under control eventually one way or the other," President Murphy predicted confidently. "In the meantime, we have our hands full rebuilding our great nation. The many directives I've enacted are a major step in that direction."

"Directives?" Donovan repeated quizzically.

"Yes. A mandatory draft of all healthy citizens is in effect. Anyone trying to flee the country will be arrested on sight. The private ownership of firearms has been outlawed and all such weapons will be confiscated. Likewise the private ownership of radio equipment is also illegal. Free enterprise has been suspended so that I can personally direct the output of our limited industrial capability. In effect, the entire country has been nationalized."

"So much for the land of the free, eh?" Captain Rockwood joked, and snickered.

Aghast at the stripping away of fundamental liberty, Donovan stared at the commander in chief. "Begging your pardon, sir, but do you have the authority to do all that?"

"Certainly," Murphy said smugly. "Haven't you heard of Executive Order 11490?"

"It rings a vague bell."

"President Richard Nixon signed the order way back in the late 1960s. It empowers the president to invoke specified emergency powers during any

155

national emergency–type situation. In effect, it the president in complete charge of every aspec daily life."

"But what about Congress and the judicial system?"

"What about them?" Murphy said, and snickered. "Maybe we'll get around to holding elections again in a hundred years or so. Until then, I and my successors will guide this country into a brand-new era."

Emotionally dazed, Donovan gazed blankly at the map. His mind boggled at the idea of the greatest democratic republic the world had ever known devolving into a pure and simple dictatorship. Now he knew with certainty that Murphy would demand that the colonists on Espiritu be brought to the United States, and under no circumstances whatsoever would he permit that to happen. But this meant he was opposing the policies of his duly designated commander. In effect, he was contemplating treason. The very word jarred him to the core of his being.

President Murphy chuckled. "You seem to be in a state of shock, Captain Donovan."

"Is it that obvious, sir?" Donovan mumbled, then shook his head to clear his thoughts and regained his presence of mind. "Sorry, but all of this is new to me. It just takes some getting used to."

"You'll adjust like everyone else," Murphy declared. "The orientation program will help immensely in that regard."

"I'm sure it will," Donovan said dryly. He noticed Rockwood staring at him with a peculiar expression; the instant he did, though, the captain's features shifted and became composed.

At that moment General Simon Hawke entered the chamber and strode directly over to the president. They spoke in hushed tones for a minute until Murphy looked at Donovan.

appears we have a bit of a problem you can help us with," the former House Speaker stated.

"I'll be glad to do anything I can."

"The officer you left in charge of *Liberator* is refusing to permit a boarding team I sent to board the submarine. I'd like for you to place a call and instruct him to mend his ways."

Donovan tensed, struggling to keep his voice level. "I'm not sure I understand, Mr. President. Why do you want a team to board my ship?"

"*Your* ship?" Murphy responded. "You seem to be forgetting yourself again, Captain. *Liberator* is part of the United States Navy. As such, she is mine to command as I see fit. You and every other member of your crew were required to take an oath of loyalty to this country when you entered the service, and I expect each and every one of you to abide by that pledge." He made a sniffing noise. "Now you will kindly speak to this Communications Officer Jennings and order him to let the boarding team on *Liberator* or else he'll find himself being court-martialed so fast it'll make his head spin."

Both the chief executive and General Hawke were staring intently at Donovan, their attitude almost hostile. He shifted uncomfortably in his seat, his mind racing, not inclined at all to grant the request but unable to come up with a logical reason to refuse it. "I'll talk to Jennings, sir," he said lamely.

"Thank you," President Murphy said, beaming. "We'll accompany you to the ComCenter. I have a few words I'd like to say to Jennings myself."

Rising, Donovan fell in behind America's new leaders. Rockwood walked to his left, deep in thought. He felt torn between his legal obligation and his commitment to his crew. But did his oath of allegiance to the United States require him to serve as cannon fodder in a dictator's insane scheme to carry on a war long since over? "If you don't mind my asking, sir," he spoke up, "what is the purpose

157

behind sending a boarding team on *Liberator!*

The president and the general exchanged quick looks, then the former answered in a condescending tone.

"There are several. First, we need to verify that all of the ship's systems are fully operational. Second, we must give all crew members a complete physical before we can transport them to Raven Rock. We need to be extremely diligent in protecting the site against the introduction of any diseases. And third, we must access all of the shipboard computer data, which means setting up an interface with our computers."

"You want to tap into the Cray-9?"

"Naturally. And I'll expect you to provide all the proper control codes."

Donovan said nothing, but he decided then and there that he wasn't about to allow Murphy access to *Liberator*'s directory. If the COG Corps tapped into the Cray-9, they would learn every detail of every system on the sub. They would know *Liberator*'s strengths and weaknesses.

They moved along a series of corridors, passing many people en route, men and women going about their daily business. The majority were dressed in the now-familiar black uniform of the COG Corps. A few bureaucratic types wore business suits. At certain junctions stood guards, each armed with an M-49, who always snapped to attention at the chief executive's approach.

Murphy glanced over his shoulder at Donovan. "Once your orientation is complete, you'll be assigned permanent quarters here. Your file states that you're single. Even so, as commander of COG's nuclear sub, you're entitled to one of the deluxe suites reserved for VIPs like us."

Donovan thought of Alex and how she would react to the idea of living in an underground bunker. She'd positively hate it. And after dwelling on Espiritu, he

...nd the prospect singularly unappealing himself.

"It's not so bad down here, Captain," General Hawke added. "The food is bland at times, we have to ration practically everything, and there's no sunshine or fresh air, but we have our own television and radio stations. For added entertainment, Site R has the largest video and CD collection in the entire world."

"Yes, indeed," President Murphy said happily. "The other night I spent close to three hours enjoying the boxed-set edition of *The Complete Madonna Collection*. Lord, that woman had a body that wouldn't quit. It's too bad she stopped making videos after she turned forty."

Visualizing the president listening to Madonna's music made Donovan laugh. He would have expected the man to go in for more highbrow stuff like Beethoven or Bach.

"Is something funny?" Murphy inquired.

"I just never imagined you would like Madonna, sir."

"I'm human, aren't I? I like a fox as much as the next man."

Oddly, General Hawke snickered as if at a private joke.

They continued until they came to double doors guarded by two corps men armed with M-49s. The general entered first and held a door open for President Murphy. Inside was an immense chamber crammed with state-of-the-art technology from the floor to the ceiling. Dozens of communications specialists were seated at various consoles or in cubicles. Another large map of the United States dominated a wall, only this one sparkled with glittering red, blue, and yellow lights.

"Right this way, Captain," General Hawke said, heading toward a console near the middle of the chamber.

159

Donovan trailed dutifully along. They'd gone ᴜ thirty feet when a harsh shout sounded in the corridor, followed by the blast of firearms. Then came a strange noise, a piercing series of high-pitched *skirrs*. It all happened in the span of seconds.

"What the hell!" General Hawke blurted, spinning and starting toward the double doors.

Suddenly those doors were flung open and in charged a man and a woman wearing the black uniforms of the COG Corps, each carrying a sonic disrupter. The man halted and bellowed: "If you move, you die!"

## 19

"How do I look?" Gloria Harrison asked.

Percy, in the act of adjusting the black belt of the COG uniform he had just donned, glanced at her and grinned. She now wore Sergeant Maxwell's uniform, which was too baggy but would have to suffice. Her blond hair contrasted sharply with the black fabric, and he found himself imagining how she would look in a black negligee.

"Well?" she prompted.

Shaking his head to dispel the vision, Percy replied, "You look like you're wearing a tent. What about me?" He had on Lieutenant Stewart's uniform, which was far too tight at the shoulders and the hips.

Gloria gave him a critical glance, then grinned. "You look as if you'll bust a seam at any second." She paused, becoming serious. "If no one looks at us too closely we should pass muster."

"It'll have to do," Percy said, and patted the .45 snug in its holster on his right hip. Then he stepped from the control room into the hallway.

Every prisoner in the detention ward had been freed. There were forty-three men, women, and children, including Randy and his sister, Janet, Duke, Maggie, and Yuma. Most wore the green gowns they had been issued upon their arrival. Three of the men, Seaman Burroughs one of them, wore COG uniforms, taken from the three guards Percy

had slain in the break room, and carried za_rr
There were also four trustees, distinguished by their yellow garb. The prisoners packed the hall on both sides, anxiously awaiting his instructions.

"You all know the risk we're taking," Percy stated without ceremony. "The odds of this plan working are slim. If we fail, there's no telling what the corps will do to us. If we succeed and I can contact my ship, and if we can arrange a rendezvous, we'll all be picked up and taken to the island I mentioned. Once we're there the corps can't touch us." He scanned their expectant faces, many of them battered and bruised. "But you don't need to go if you don't want to. Those who would rather stay here are welcome to return to their cells."

An elderly woman shuffled forward. "Young man, I think I'd like to stay. I'm not up to a lot of running or fighting. And although I know these COG people are real turds, I'd rather take my chances with them."

"As you wish," Percy said. "Go on back to your cell and we'll lock you in."

"Thank you," the woman said, and walked off.

"Anyone else?" Percy asked. "Now's the time to speak up. We've got to set our plan in motion." He glanced into the control room at the monitors on the wall, at the pair of screens Gloria had pointed out to him earlier as being linked to cameras situated near the two entrances into the ward. So far luck had been with them and no one had appeared, no alarms had sounded. Evidently internal monitoring of the ward was considered sufficient security; none of the cameras were hooked to corps stations elsewhere in Raven Rock.

Seaman Burroughs stepped over, his face bearing multiple bruises, and pointed the zapper he held at the two furious men seated on the corridor floor just to the right of the control room door. "What are we going to do with these two, sir?"

162

ve them to me," one of the prisoners declared. "I owe those sons of bitches for the way they treated me."

Percy stared at Lieutenant Stewart and Sergeant Maxwell. Both men now wore green prisoner garb. Both had their wrists bound behind their backs. And both were glaring malevolently at him. "We're taking them with us," he announced.

A murmur rippled among the prisoners.

"Why the hell should we risk it?" a man demanded to know.

"Because we need them," Percy admitted, and gazed at the anxious faces to his right and left. "We can't just waltz out of the detention ward, grab the first vehicles we find, and head for the surface. We need a diversion, something to keep the corps preoccupied while we make our escape. And if we can disrupt their command control network, so much the better." He paused. "There must be a communications center somewhere in this complex. These men will take us to it."

"Like hell we will!" Lieutenant Stewart snapped.

"Never happen, bastard," Maxwell added.

Sighing, Percy drew his Colt, cocked the hammer, and touched the cold tip of the barrel to the officer's forehead. "I have nothing to lose by killing you right here and now. If you refuse to cooperate, then I'll splatter your brains all over the wall."

Gloria drew Maxwell's sidearm, smirked at the sergeant, and before anyone could suspect her intent rammed the barrel into his stomach. He doubled over, wheezing. "The same goes for you, you miserable son of a bitch," she said harshly. "Give me an excuse, *any* excuse, and I'll kill the both of you and hang the consequences."

"I'd listen to her, gentlemen," Percy said, suppressing a grin. "You saw what she did to your friend Lamar."

Lieutenant Stewart stared at her, his cracked,

puffy lips twitching. He focused on the .45, glanced at the wheezing sergeant. "We don't have any choice. We'll have to do as they say."

"But sir—" Maxwell protested.

"What harm can it do?" Stewart told his subordinate. "They'll never get out of the bunker."

Percy straightened and holstered the Colt. "As I was saying," he said loud enough for everyone to hear, "there must be a communications center in Raven Rock. If we find it, I can radio my captain to arrange a pickup. Then we'll put the center out of commission and get the hell out of here."

"We're with you," a woman assured him. "Just lead the way."

"First things first," Percy responded. "We can't straggle through the halls or we'll be stopped by the first guards we encounter. I've already told you how we'll play this, so let's get organized." He placed his hands on his hips and watched as the prisoners formed into a double file. His plan was simple. They were going to pretend that a bunch of guards were escorting a group of prisoners somewhere and hope no one questioned them too closely. "Burroughs, I want you and the other two men wearing uniforms to walk beside the prisoners. Assign one man to the rear, another a third of the way up, and you walk near the head of the column. Gloria and I will be at the front with these two fascists." He jabbed a thumb at the officer and the noncom.

"Yes, sir," the crewman said, and went about relaying the instructions to the pair of prisoners in black.

"Hey, what about us, Mr. Percy?" asked Janet.

"We want to stay near you," Randy chimed in.

"No problem," Percy said, smiling, relieved that neither of them had been brutalized. Children, apparently, were exempt from the grueling interrogation sessions and were actually treated decently. "You can stay right behind Gloria and me."

164

_____ he your wife?" Randy inquired in all inno-
cence.

Taken aback, Percy glanced at Gloria, who had
unaccountably turned crimson, and chuckled. "No.
We're just good friends."

"Maybe you should marry her when we get out of
here," Randy said. "My dad told me that every man
should have a wife."

"I'll keep it in mind," Percy said dryly, and coughed
to clear his throat. He scanned the line of prisoners,
satisfied with the arrangement. Then he faced the
corps men. "On your feet."

Stewart and Maxwell rose awkwardly, using the
wall for support since they couldn't use their hands
to push upright. The noncom's eyes blazed hatred.

Percy pursed his lips, reflecting. He wouldn't put
it past Maxwell to try to alert any corps members they passed in the corridors to what was going
down. One shout was all it would take. He decided
to leave Maxwell behind; they didn't really need
both interrogators. Pivoting, he caught Burroughs's
eye and motioned for the crewman to come over.

"Yes, sir?"

"Find a gown or something you can tear into
strips. Then take Sergeant Maxwell back into the
break room, bind his legs, and gag him. If he gives
you any trouble, use your zapper on him."

"With pleasure," Burroughs said, grinning, and
hastened toward one of the cells.

Maxwell leaned toward Percy. "You prick!"

To Percy's surprise, Gloria hauled off and kicked
the sergeant in the groin. Maxwell doubled over, his
face becoming beet red.

"Not another word out of you," she snapped.

Tough lady, Percy mused, and walked along the
line of prisoners, offering encouragement, telling
them they would all get out of Raven Rock in one
piece if they stuck together. The anxious looks they
bestowed on him, as if he was their last hope in the

165

world, struck a responsive chord in the dep̶̶
his being. By the time he returned to the head of
the column Sergeant Maxwell was gone and Seaman Burroughs stood near the control room door,
smirking.

"I took care of it, sir. Had to use the zapper,
though."

"Okay. Take your position," Percy ordered. He
stepped up to Lieutenant Stewart, grabbed the man
by the front of the gown, and jerked him to a spot a
few feet from the wall. "You'll walk between Gloria
and me. One peep and you're dead."

Gloria touched her pistol. "*Please* make a peep. I
love wasting you sadistic cruds."

The officer shook his head. "Don't worry. I'll do
whatever you want. I'm not about to get myself
killed."

Percy glanced at Gloria. "That reminds me. Will
you lock that elderly woman into her cell? We don't
want her getting into trouble on our account."

Nodding, Gloria went into the control room.

The prisoners waited nervously for her to emerge,
speaking in whispers. Many fidgeted. A few bit their
nails.

At last Gloria came out. "She's lying on her cot,
snug and safe."

"Then let's get this show on the road," Percy said.
He gave Stewart a shove in the direction they were
headed and began walking down the hall. The rest
of the prisoners promptly followed. "I thought you
corps types were supposed to be the cream of the
crop," he said to the officer. "Aren't you required
to give your life for COG? Where's your devotion to
duty now?"

"Duty is one thing," Stewart said. "My ass is
another. I'd rather live to fight another day than
get blown away for no reason."

"In other words, you're a damn coward," Gloria said.

166

"...re only tough when you have the upper hand."

The officer made no reply.

They came to a junction and took a right. Ahead were solid wooden double doors leading from the detention ward into the complex proper.

"Are guards posted outside the ward?" Percy inquired.

"Yes," Stewart stated. "Two. One on each side of the corridor."

"Firearms?"

"M16s."

They drew within ten feet of the entrance. Percy halted and everyone else did the same. "Keep him covered," he said to Gloria, who promptly drew her .45 and jammed the barrel into Stewart's back. He faced front, strode briskly to the swinging doors, and shoved the right one wide open.

There stood the guards, brawny men in black who snapped to attention the instant he appeared. M16s were slung over their right shoulders.

"I need some help in here," Percy stated, and started to draw back before either man could question the order. The officer's insignia on his uniform did the trick. Both soldiers hurried inside to render aid. He courteously held the door until they went by, then drew his pistol and trained the Colt on them as they halted in surprise.

"What is this?" one of them blurted.

"Trick or treat," Percy quipped, smiling when they looked at him, their eyes widening at the sight of his pistol. "Now be so kind as to hand your rifles over and take off your uniforms."

"You're nuts," declared the other guard. "We'll do no such thing."

Gloria moved a step away from Lieutenant Stewart and held her Colt in a two-handed grip, her arms steady, aiming at the speaker, her tone mocking as she said, "Suit yourselves, boys. But as

167

soon as you twitch I'm going to blow your balls.

The guards looked at one another, at the prisoners, then at the blond woman calmly awaiting their decision. In unison they let their M16s slide to the floor.

"Smart move," Percy complimented them, sliding forward to scoop the rifles up by the slings. He kept his .45 trained on the duo as they slowly removed their uniforms.

Seaman Burroughs hurried up and pointed at the pile of clothes. "Should I issue these to two prisoners, sir?"

"You've got it," Percy replied, extending the M16s. "Issue one of the rifles also, but keep the other one for yourself."

"What about my zapper?"

"Give it to the second man who receives a uniform. The more prisoners who are armed, the better our chances."

"Yes, sir," Burroughs said. He took the uniforms and the M16s and hastened back along the line.

Smirking, Gloria wagged her pistol at the guards, who now sheepishly stood in their underwear. "What about these two hunks?"

"Give them a taste of the accommodations here," Percy directed, and waited while she took them to the nearest empty cell, pushed them both inside, and pressed the black button on the wall to close the door. He admired her no-nonsense professionalism and thought to pose a question when she rejoined him. "Say, what did you do before the war, anyway?"

"I was a cop."

"Explains a lot," Percy said, and stepped up to Stewart. "The next step of this operation depends on you. If you screw up, you won't live to brag about it." He paused. "You're going to take us to the communications center by the shortest possible route. Since you must know the layout of Raven

168

...by heart, I would suggest that you pick corridors where there won't be any guards and where the traffic will be light. If we're stopped, I'll do the talking. Any questions?"

"No," the officer answered sullenly. "I'll do what you want. It will take us about ten minutes to get there, and I think I can avoid the guard stations."

"You *think*?" Gloria repeated.

Stewart ignored her. "I should warn you that there are guards posted right outside the Com-Center. There's no way we can avoid them."

"We'll deal with that situation when we get there," Percy said, and took the officer by the upper arm. "Now let's go." He gazed at the prisoners. "This is it, people. Keep quiet and remember to act the way prisoners should act. Keep your heads down as if you're miserable. If one of you cracks a smile and someone should see it, we'd arouse suspicion." He made for the entrance, tugging Stewart along with him, keeping the Colt hidden behind the officer's back. Despite the man's stated intention to cooperate, he didn't trust Stewart one bit.

But the COG officer turned out to be as good as his word. Lieutenant Stewart guided them along a veritable maze of passageways, sticking to sparsely frequented corridors, taking a right turn here, a left turn there. They still encountered a couple of dozen people, all of whom went their way without giving the column of prisoners so much as a second glance. And the majority of the people wore black uniforms.

Percy tensed at the sight of the first pair, two women strolling casually along while conversing in subdued tones. Neither was armed. He glanced at Stewart. "What gives? Are they soldiers?"

"No," the officer said. "Probably secretaries, since we're in the lower Admin level."

"Then why are they wearing uniforms?"

"Didn't I make myself clear? All citizens are being

169

mustered into COG. Everyone except a few bureaucratic types wears COG uniforms, and even they will before too long, I bet." He nodded toward the approaching women. "Soldiers wear military insignia and chevrons, civilians don't. Any dummy can tell the difference."

"Don't push your luck," Percy advised, relieved at the news.

They were almost to their destination when they ran into a trooper, a lone soldier with an M16 over his shoulder, heading in the opposite direction. The man stiffened at the sight of Percy and snapped off a salute as he went by. Otherwise, he displayed no interest in the column.

Percy's confidence grew by leaps and bounds the farther they went without being challenged. The COG Corps wasn't infallible. The very discipline instilled in the troops worked against them. A typical grunt wasn't about to question a superior officer, so unless they ran into someone of higher rank than a lieutenant Percy believed he could bluff his way into the ComCenter without any difficulty. A minute later his belief was put to the test.

They took a left at the next corner. Situated halfway down the corridor were double doors guarded by a pair of corps troopers. Slung over their shoulders were unusual black machine guns sporting peculiar spheres at the ends of the barrels.

"There's the ComCenter," Lieutenant Stewart announced.

Peeved that the officer hadn't let him know they were almost there, Percy jammed the Colt into the base of Stewart's spine. "Just remember you'll be the first one to go if you open your mouth."

Stewart's features hardened. Then he gazed at the two men on guard duty and his eyes danced with mirth.

Percy squared his shoulders and adopted an appropriately stern expression. If he gave the

. s the impression he was a hardass, they'd be less likely to give him any trouble. Both troopers snapped to attention at his approach. He drew to a stop a few feet from them and barked, "Detail, halt!"

The column abruptly did so.

"Sergeant Harrison," Percy said to Gloria, "make sure these prisoners keep quiet while I'm in the ComCenter." He went to take a step, intending to whip the Colt from concealment and cover the guards while she disarmed them. But one of the troopers, who until that very instant had been staring straight ahead, glanced out of the corner of his eyes and saw Stewart.

The soldier blinked, then swung around, beginning to unsling his weapon, his brow knitting. "Lieutenant Stewart? Is that you, sir? What's going on here?"

Stewart suddenly slid toward the wall and bellowed, "It's an escape attempt! Kill them!"

Both guards tried to bring their strange guns into play.

Since Percy already had the .45 clutched in his hand, it was a simple matter for him to snap off a shot into the first guard's chest. Gloria added her firepower to the fray, shooting the second trooper. The two men went down, the first one still game though. On his back, propped on his elbows, blood spurting from the hole in his chest, he valiantly tried to aim the weird machine gun. Percy shot him again for good measure.

The man was flattened by the close-range impact, but as he died his trigger finger convulsively tightened and the weapon in his hands went off. Instead of a shot, a shrill series of electronic-sounding shrieks filled the air, emanating from the odd sphere at the end of the barrel. At the moment the weapon fired, it was angled upward and to the right, pointing directly at Lieutenant Stewart.

171

The officer opened his mouth to scream, his
wide with terror. A heartbeat later the incredible
occurred: his chest literally exploded. A circular section four inches in diameter simply burst outward
like an overripe melon, showering flesh and blood
and gore all over the floor.

Percy instinctively recognized a godsend when he
saw one. He was in motion even before Stewart
sagged to the floor, holstering the Colt and stepping
forward to yank the strange weapon from the dead
guard's hand. Gloria darted to the second guard and
took that trooper's black blaster. They exchanged
glances. He grinned, said "Let's go for it," and barged
through the double doors with her at his side.

**20**

Recognition dawned an instant after the man in the corps uniform burst into the chamber and shouted his warning. Astonished, Donovan blurted out, "Percy!"

The executive officer was in the act of scanning the communications center, his weapon levelled, his finger on the trigger. His eyes alighted on Donovan and widened in amazement. "Captain!"

Donovan beamed and took a step toward his friend, then froze when the blond woman accompanying Percy trained her M-49 on him and barked an order.

"Didn't you hear the man, clunkhead? Don't move!"

Percy glanced at her. "It's all right. He's on our side."

So far none of the personnel in the ComCenter had so much as moved. Suddenly several came to life. A man seated at a console on the right opened a drawer and whipped out a pistol. Off to the left two unarmed corps members sprinted toward Percy and the woman.

"Look out!" Donovan shouted.

Percy had already seen the guy with the pistol. He fired, the M-49 shrieking like a banshee, and the man at the console screamed as his chest ruptured in a shower of flesh and blood.

The blonde was equally alert. She swept her son~~~
disrupter around to cover the onrushing duo and
called out, "Stop or die!"

Neither one slowed.

"Suit yourselves," the blonde said, and blasted
them both. They reacted as if they'd slammed into
an invisible wall, halting with their arms outflung,
their torsos exploding. Both fell where they stood.
She swept the M-49 around the chamber and yelled,
"Does anyone else feel like being a hero?"

No one apparently did.

President Murphy finally found his voice. "What is
the meaning of this outrage?" he demanded angrily.
"Who are you two? You'll be court-martialed for this
atrocity."

"And who might you be?" Percy asked, coming
over to stand in front of Donovan.

The blonde stayed right beside him, covering his
back and sides, her eyes darting right and left.

Donovan jerked a thumb at the chief executive.
"This is President Murphy, the new commander in
chief. He arranged a meeting with me and then
brought me here to discuss his plans to rebuild
America." He paused, glancing from his executive
officer to the woman. "John, what the hell is going
on? How did you get here? Who's your new friend?"

"This is Gloria Harrison," Percy introduced her
while surveying the ComCenter. Then he looked at
Donovan. "Captain, we've got to get out of Raven
Rock. I don't have time to go into detail, but there
are close to four dozen survivors waiting out in the
hallway. We've all just escaped from the detention
ward here."

"You've *what*?" President Murphy bellowed before
Donovan could respond. "How dare you!" He nodded
at the general. "Surrender yourselves to General
Hawke immediately."

"Shut up, idiot," Gloria snapped.

Murphy bristled and shook a fist at her. "I'm

President of the United States, young woman. You will address me with the respect my office deserves."

"Whatever you want, moron," Gloria said, and swung the stock of her M-49 in a vicious arc, clipping Murphy on the jaw. The chief executive's eyelids fluttered and he fell in a heap. Gloria glanced down at him and frowned. "What a wimp."

"We have no time for this," Percy said, anxiously surveying the chamber. When no one made a move, he faced Donovan again. "Believe me, sir. If we don't haul butt right this minute, none of us may get out of Site R alive." He wagged his weapon at General Hawke. "These COG bozos are nothing but cut-rate fascists. They're capturing all survivors and forcibly relocating them here to restock the labor pool. Individual freedom no longer exists and everyone is treated like cattle." He scowled. "The government has gone completely haywire."

Donovan listened attentively. Percy wasn't telling him anything he didn't already know. But now he was confronted with the harsh necessity of making a decision, perhaps the most momentous decision of his entire life. If he sided with his executive officer and assisted the survivors in escaping, he was essentially severing all ties, legal and moral, with the United States government; he was committing treason. But if he tried to talk Percy out of fleeing, if he allowed his crew to be brainwashed by the COG Corps and surrendered all the colonists on Espiritu to COG control, he would be a traitor to them and to himself. He had only seconds to make up his mind. Which would it be? Stick by his oath of allegiance to the United States of America even though the government that had been in existence at the time he made the oath no longer existed, or abide by a higher, ethical, personal obligation that required him to own up to his responsibility to his crew and to the colonists who depended on him to safeguard their lives and liberty? There was really no cho

"Sir?" Percy prompted.

"Let's go," Donovan directed. He indicated the president and the general. "We'll take these two along as hostages and try to reach *Liberator*. I doubt we'll be attacked as long as we have them in our custody."

Percy glanced at Gloria. "Get Burroughs on the double. Tell him to bring two others."

Without a word she raced to the double doors.

Donovan looked at Captain Rockwood. "You'll be coming with us also, Drew."

The officer, judging by his expression, was in emotional turmoil. He stared at the prone president, then at Donovan. "Why me?"

"You'll be in charge of the Dragonflies that will fly all the survivors to *Liberator*."

"I'd rather not."

"It wasn't a request," Donovan noted.

General Hawke, who until that moment had been strangely silent, although his malevolent features eloquently displayed his feelings, finally interjected a remark while staring at Rockwood. "You are to keep all Dragonflies on the ground. Do you understand me, Captain?"

Donovan stepped up to the general and jabbed a finger into Hawke's chest. "You don't have a say in this, mister."

Hawke ignored him. "This is a direct order, Captain Rockwood. Under no circumstances whatsoever are you to transport these seditionists from Raven Rock."

"Seditionists?" Percy said, and snorted.

The double doors swung open and in came Gloria Harrison, Seaman Burroughs, and two male prisoners. Burroughs saw Donovan and grinned from ear to ear.

"Captain! It's great to see you again! What are you doing here?"

176

ll explain later," Donovan said. He indicated the two prisoners. "Would you gentleman pick up President Murphy and bring him along?"

They complied without question.

Donovan held out his right hand to Percy. "Let me have that Colt."

"Here you go, sir," the executive officer said, handing it over.

Hefting the .45 for a moment, Donovan suddenly cocked it and touched the barrel to General Hawke's forehead. "I want to call my ship. Take me to the proper console."

The general frowned but made no comment. He moved to the left and stopped beside a communications specialist seated in front of a bank of high-tech gear. "This private can place the call."

Donovan swung the pistol to cover the specialist. "Raise *Liberator*. Use a secure channel."

The man nodded and went to reach for a button.

"If you try to trick me, if you don't use a secure channel, I'll know," Donovan warned gruffly.

Glancing at the Colt, the specialist hesitated, then pressed a different button and spoke into a microphone. "Site R to U.S.S. *Liberator*, come in please. Site R to U.S.S. *Liberator*, do you copy?"

Static crackled from a speaker mounted high on the console, and then a familiar voice acknowledged the transmission.

"Site R, this is U.S.S. *Liberator*, Communications Officer Jennings speaking. I'm still waiting to speak with my captain. Where is he? Over."

Donovan leaned forward and stabbed the proper button. "I'm right here, Dave. I've got no time to explain, so listen closely. You are not—repeat, *not*—to let the Raven Rock boarding team on *Liberator*. Percy and I are on our way back and we're bringing over forty survivors with us. I want to get under way the minute I'm on board. Did you get all that?"

"Yes, sir," Jennings replied.

"If you're attacked before we arrive, you are to fight back. If you think you can't hold out, get out of there. Over."

"We're not leaving without you, Skipper."

"Don't argue." Donovan looked at the communications specialist. "And tell me. Is this call on a secure channel?"

"Affirmative."

"Okay. Sound Alert Stations immediately. Donovan out." He straightened and escorted General Hawke back to where the others were anxiously waiting. "Let's get going," he proposed. "Mr. Percy, will you and Ms. Harrison do the honors and take care of this ComCenter?"

"With pleasure," the executive officer replied.

They set their escape into motion. Donovan and Burroughs escorted General Hawke and Captain Rockwood to the corridor. The two prisoners hauled President Murphy out.

Percy and Gloria ordered the communications personnel to line up against a wall. While Gloria covered them, Percy hastily went from console to console and gave each a short burst of the sonic disrupter. Although he didn't quite comprehend the principle behind the weapon, he figured that any rifle capable of blowing a human chest apart would wreak utter havoc with sensitive electronic circuits, and he turned out to be right. The disrupter caused casings to split, wires to short-circuit, and sparks and flames to flare from the equipment. By the time he finished a hazy cloud of acrid smoke was forming and the ComCenter was effectively out of commission. He ran to the double doors, paused until Gloria joined him, and together they backed out.

President Murphy had just revived. He stood under his own power, swaying slightly, rubbing his sore jaw, and glared at Gloria.

All done, Skipper," Percy announced.

Donovan walked up to the chief executive and trained the Colt on Murphy's stomach. "You're going to lead us safely out of Raven Rock."

"Dream on, Donovan."

Gloria abruptly stepped forward and pointed her M-49 at the president's head. "Say the word, Captain Donovan, and this son of a bitch is history."

Murphy blinked, impressed by her vehemence. "You would, wouldn't you?"

"After the sheer hell your lousy corps put me through?" Gloria rejoined. "Gladly."

Donovan glanced both ways along the corridor. There was no sign of Site R Security yet, but it was only a matter of time. "What's it going to be, Murphy? Either you take us to the surface or she kills you."

The former House Speaker nervously chewed on his lower lip. He looked at Hawke, who shook his head, then at Gloria's M-49. "All right, bastard. I'll do as you say."

"Figured you would," Donovan said. "Take us to the parking facility. We'll need vehicles. And remember, if we're stopped by soldiers you'd better convince them to stand aside or you'll be one of the first to die."

"Don't worry on that score," Murphy snapped. "I want to live to see you tried for high treason and then duly sentenced to death. We have an electric chair here, you know, for recalcitrant criminals like yourself."

"I'm sure you do," Donovan said, and gestured with the .45. "Now lead the way."

President Murphy glowered but obeyed. They proceeded to the next junction, then took a left. No sooner had they done so than a general alarm sounded, with sirens going off all over the installation. Murphy halted and looked at Donovan. "Why don't you save yourself a lot of unnecessary grief and

179

give up? You don't stand a chance against the ⟨
Corps."

"Just keep walking," Donovan said, jabbing the
Colt into Murphy's side.

Clearly exasperated, the chief executive continued
their flight. The sirens kept blaring. Soon they
encountered corps personnel hurrying to and fro,
ducking into offices on either side. Then, up ahead,
appeared a half-dozen armed troopers.

Donovan stood directly behind Murphy and
watched the squad approach. The man in the lead
raised his right hand and stopped when only twenty
feet away.

"Mr. President, sir!"

"Sergeant Kunze, isn't it?" Murphy responded.

"Yes, sir." Kunze gazed past the president at the
column. "General Hawke? What's going on here,
sir? Why has the alarm sounded? And what are
those prisoners doing out of the detention ward?"

Donovan raised the pistol for the squad to see,
the barrel touching Murphy's ear. "We're holding
the president and General Hawke as hostages. If
you interfere, they die."

"What the—!" Kunze blurted, and began to bring
an M16 into play. He checked his motion, however,
and stared at Murphy. "What do we do, sir?"

"You go find Major General Rainey," Murphy
directed. "Tell him what you've seen. Tell him that
I'm guiding escaped prisoners and Captain Thomas
Donovan from the U.S.S. *Liberator* to Parking Level
B. Tell him—and this is a direct order—he is not
to do anything for the time being. He is not to
attack, not to hinder these people in any way. Do
you understand?"

"Yes, sir."

"Haul ass, Sergeant."

Kunze whirled and led his squad back along the
corridor.

"Well done," Donovan complimented Murphy

..le giving him a slight shove. "Let's head out."

The next ten minutes dragged by as if weighted with anchors. Palpable tension hung in the air. The survivors were silent, radiating anxiety. The farther they traveled, the fewer personnel they saw.

Donovan guessed that COG soldiers were clearing the corridors. He doubted the corps would spring an ambush, but every time he passed a closed door his spine tingled. The sirens wailed the entire time, a constant reminder that death might lurk around the next corner. A wave of relief washed over him after rounding yet another corner when he spied an unoccupied mahogany desk and double doors a few dozen yards away. "Is that the parking level?" he asked.

"Yes," Murphy confirmed. "I hope you're happy."

"I won't be happy until I'm back on my ship," Donovan said. He glanced at Percy. "Take the point. Peek through those doors and make sure there are no nasty surprises on the other side."

"Yes, sir," Percy replied, sprinting forward.

Without being told or asked, Gloria Harrison went with him.

President Murphy bestowed a scornful glare on Donovan. "You realize, don't you, that there isn't a place on Earth where you'll be safe from my retribution? If it takes the rest of my life, I'll see that you're hunted down and made to pay for this heinous affront to the country you were sworn to defend at all costs."

"This isn't the country I swore to protect. America is gone and so is her duly elected government. Freedom and democracy are no more," Donovan said bitterly. "COG is a travesty of everything America stood for. And you're not a president; you're a dictator."

"Is this how you justify your treason? With noble platitudes?"

Donovan knew it would be a waste of time to

181

debate the point. He saw Percy and Gloria ru_ the doors. His X.O. cracked one and scanned the parking level, then both raced back to report.

"There are all kinds of vehicles," Percy said, "but there isn't a soul anywhere."

"Good. I remember seeing convoy trucks earlier. We'll load everyone into two or three and head for the surface," Donovan proposed.

"What about the keys?" Gloria asked.

From Seaman Burroughs, who was covering Hawke and Rockwood, came a chuckle. "Don't worry on that score. I worked as a mechanic at my uncle's garage when I was in high school. I can jump start anything with wheels."

"So can I," chimed in one of the prisoners.

"We may need you to," Donovan told them. Taking the lead, he hastened past the doors and paused to survey the parking facility, the rest eagerly filing out behind him. The convoy trucks were right where he'd seen them. As he gazed to the right and left, he noticed a black telephone mounted on the wall near the doors. He went over, picked it up, and was pleased to hear a dial tone. Evidently knocking out the ComCenter hadn't disrupted all of the phone service. "Come here, Murphy," he directed the chief executive.

Reluctantly, the president came over. "What is it now?"

"When we landed I saw four choppers on a pad. If the one we came in is still up there, that would make five, more than enough to transport us to *Liberator*. Use this phone and contact Major General Rainey. Tell him I want all five Dragonflies ready to lift off the second we reach them. And the only personnel on those aircraft had better be the pilots or you know what will happen. Got that?"

"Loud and clear," Murphy said sullenly.

"Then get cracking," Donovan ordered, and handed over the phone. He turned to Percy.

182

nn, get all the survivors into convoy trucks. we shouldn't need to take more than two if we pack them in like sardines. Then start the trucks and wait for me."

"Yes, sir," Percy said, and started to pivot.

"Oh. Keep General Hawke and Captain Rockwood out until last. We want them near the back in case the corps opens fire."

Nodding his comprehension, Percy hustled off. His blond shadow accompanied him.

Donovan turned and listened to President Murphy relay the demands to Rainey. Thankfully, Rainey didn't argue. These corps types, he reflected, were as well trained as German shepherd attack dogs. When Murphy finished, Donovan escorted him across the parking level to the trucks. Most of the survivors were already on board and the man who had said he could jump start vehicles was doing so.

Burroughs stood next to the tailgate of the lead truck, his M16 trained on the general and Rockwood.

The first vehicle rumbled to life. Immediately the man slammed the hood down and went to the second truck.

"We're just about set, Captain," Percy announced, coming over.

"Then put General Hawke at the rear of the second truck. You can ride with him. If we're attacked, shoot him."

"With great pleasure," Percy said, pointing the M-49 at the general. "After you."

Donovan watched them go, Gloria at Percy's side, then motioned for President Murphy to climb up into the bed of the first vehicle. "Your chariot awaits, your highness."

Murphy became beet red with indignation. "You'll pay, Donovan. Oh, *how* you'll pay."

"I thought you didn't like platitudes."

"Screw you."

In short order everyone was in a truck. Burrou
took the wheel of the lead vehicle; the man who ha
started them both got into the cab of the second.

Donovan gave each man specific instructions.
They were to stick to the center of the road and
under no circumstances were they to stop until
they were at the landing pad on top of the hill. If
they saw a roadblock, they were to lean on the horn
and crash right through. He walked to the rear of
the first truck and climbed up beside Murphy and
Rockwood. "Comfy, gentlemen?"

Neither man bothered to answer.

At a shout from Donovan the two trucks moved
out, their normally loud engines sounding even
louder in the subterranean parking complex, the
noise they made amplified by the walls and ceiling.
He pointed the Colt at Murphy and tried to relax,
but his nerves refused to cooperate. So far, so good,
he noted. If they made it up the long tunnel without
being ambushed, and if there weren't snipers posted
on top to gun them down when they hopped off the
trucks, and if the Dragonfly pilots didn't pull any
devious stunts, he might well live to reach *Liberator*.
If. If. If. Sometimes he hated that word.

As it turned out, the barrier gates at each checkpoint were open and there was no sign of corps
troopers. The trucks traveled unmolested all the
way to the surface. When the vehicles finally
emerged into the sunlight, the prisoners in both
vented spontaneous cheers.

Donovan wasn't about to cheer until he stood
on his bridge again. He glanced toward the gate
and saw the two squads still guarding it, but the
men were standing at attention with their weapons
slung, a clear indication they had received instructions not to interfere. He grinned at them as the
truck began to climb the road to the top.

Leaning out the side, Donovan strained for a
glimpse of the landing pad. When at last he saw

ive helicopters, their rotors spinning in preparation for taking off, he almost whooped for joy. Rather than get cocky, he sat down and looked at the president. "I want you to know I never meant for it to turn out this way. I would much rather be your ally than your enemy. But as long as you persist in riding roughshod over the survivors, as long as you think you have the right to trample innocent lives under your heel just to rebuild America the way you see fit, we'll be at odds."

"Don't attempt to justify your treason, mister," Murphy said. "From this moment forth you can consider yourself a renegade, an outcast officially at war with the United States of America. You might have a nuclear sub at your disposal, but we have a few surprises of our own up our sleeve. We'll find you and send you down to join the *Deutschland* at the bottom of the ocean."

"This is insane. We should be working together to salvage what's left of civilization."

"The only civilization that counts is the good old U. S. of A. Apparently you've forgotten where your loyalties should lie."

Donovan gave it up. He noticed Rockwood regarding him thoughtfully and went to ask the reason when the trucks abruptly braked at the landing pad. Two prisoners quickly let down the tailgate and Donovan jumped to the ground.

There were no corps personnel anywhere around.

Working swiftly, Donovan divided the survivors into five groups and saw that each group got safely on board a chopper. Percy and Gloria took General Hawke on one. Donovan kept scanning the hill, half expecting marksmen to open fire from concealment, but nothing happened. He couldn't quite believe the ease with which the escape was being accomplished. It made him suspect that the corps held a trump card they had yet to play.

Into the last Dragonfly, the one that had brought

185

Donovan to Raven Rock, piled Burroughs, five
vivors, the chief executive, Captain Rockwood, and
finally Donovan himself. He closed the cockpit door
and squatted beside it. Since there was only seating
for six, he had to make do.

The pilot looked over his shoulder, resentment
lining his features. "We're exceeding our weight
capacity," he commented.

"We'll get by," Donovan said. "These things are
powerful enough to lift a tank. Just take it a bit
slower than usual and we'll reach our destination
intact."

"What is our destination, if I may ask?"

"Blakistone Island. Lift off immediately."

"Yes, sir," the pilot said, turning to his controls.

In a twinkling they were airborne. Donovan
braced his back against the door and did something
he hadn't done in ages.

He prayed.

"E.T.A. is two minutes," the pilot announced.

Donovan rose into a crouch and scooted forward to squat next to the man. "How far away are we?"

"Two hundred and forty miles."

Well beyond transceiver range. "I want to talk to my ship," Donovan stated.

The pilot looked back at President Murphy, who glumly nodded, then handed his headset over. "I'll press the transmit button when you give the word."

Donning the headset, Donovan adjusted the mouthpiece and nodded. "Go ahead." He saw the man stab a button and heard crackling in his ears. "Red One to *Liberator*. Do you copy?"

Less than two seconds elapsed before Jennings replied. "Picking you up loud and clear, sir. Where are you?"

"We're en route to the island in five Dragonflies. We'll be there in under two minutes. What's your status?"

"It's been as calm as could be. The helicopters that were keeping watch over this stretch of the river flew off about fifteen minutes ago and haven't returned."

Donovan pursed his lips. Where could the Dragonflies have gone? Had Rainey called them off? If so, why? "All right. Listen up. I want every inflatable we have rowed to the island right away. We must get

the survivors on the ship as quickly as possible. _ _
stay glued to your monitors and let me know if radar
shows anything heading in our direction."

"Anything else?"

"Is the Walther manned? Are the lasers in weapons mode?"

"We're on Full Alert status, as you ordered."

"Then we're as ready as we're going to be. Donovan
out." He gave the headset to the pilot and moved
back to the door. Blakistone Island appeared ahead.
In virtually no time they were hovering over the
beach on the south side. Donovan felt his pulse
quicken at the sight of *Liberator*'s teal-colored hull
glistening in the bright sunlight, and he longed to be
back on board with Alex. There were crewmen scurrying about on the foredeck, preparing inflatables
for launch. The gun crew had the Walther trained in
the general direction of the shore. "Take us down at
the water's edge," he commanded the corps pilot.

The man frowned but obeyed, setting the chopper
down as gently as a feather settling to the earth
within six yards of the Potomac. He flicked a toggle
to kill the rotors and swiveled in his chair. "What
now, mister?"

Donovan saw the other helicopters landing on
either side. "Radio those pilots and tell them to stay
in their seats. And keep your choppers grounded
until I give you the all clear." He stood, opened the
cockpit door, and jumped to the sand.

A familiar figure standing on *Liberator*'s topside
bridge saw him and waved.

Beaming, Donovan did the same. Then he devoted himself to the task of getting all the survivors
off the helicopters and grouped close to the river.
Several inflatables were already on their way from
the sub. He walked over to where Percy, Gloria, and
Burroughs were guarding the hostages.

"I suppose you think you've won," President Murphy said.

. not trying to win anything," Donovan corrected him. "I'm trying to get out of here in one piece."

"You'll never make it," Murphy predicted.

Percy took a step forward. "What are we going to do with these three, Captain?"

"I vote we waste them," Gloria said.

"We're not murderers," Donovan said. "We don't kill people in cold blood. These three were our ticket out of Raven Rock. Once we're all on *Liberator*, we won't need them anymore."

"You're going to let these scumbags live?" Gloria asked in amazement.

Donovan nodded and faced the river, unwilling to debate the issue. He might live to regret his decision, but he wouldn't stoop so low as to slay three unarmed men, especially when one of those men was the president. Old habits were hard to break, and although he knew Murphy was in the wrong, he couldn't entirely cast off his ingrained deference to the position itself. The very idea of murdering a president was almost unthinkable.

The first three inflatables were nearly to the island. One of them put in near Donovan and a crewman brought over a Franchi. "Mr. Jennings thought you might need this, sir."

"Thanks," Donovan said, and slung it over his left shoulder. He unclipped the transceiver from his belt and switched it on. "Red One to *Liberator*. Status update."

"There's been no change, Skipper," Jennings answered. "Nothing on radar at all."

"Are you monitoring the broadcast spectrum?"

"Of course. The computer is scanning every frequency, but there hasn't been a peep out of the corps."

"They're up to something. I can feel it in my bones," Donovan said. "Keep me posted." He turned to Percy. "Start transferring the survivors to the

189

ship and get them below. Have the inflatable c̶ r̶

return to the island immediately after dropping off
each load. We're like sitting ducks here on this
beach and I don't like it one bit."

Percy glanced skyward. "You're not the only one."
With Gloria in tow he began issuing instructions to
the assembled prisoners.

A low snicker brought Donovan around to stare
at the chief executive. "What's so funny?"

"You are," Murphy said. "You can't hope to escape
us."

"That remains to be seen," Donovan said, and
gazed at the other two. Neither General Hawke
nor Rockwood had said very much since they were
taken captive at the ComCenter. The general, in
particular, had strangely clammed up. Why? Simple resentment at being taken prisoner? Or was
Hawke deliberately trying to avoid doing anything
that would draw attention to himself? Again, if so,
why? He studied the man's glaring features for a
bit, then happened to notice the twin pockets on
the general's shirt. The right-hand pocket bulged
slightly with the telltale outline of a small notebook
or tablet. "What's that you've got in your pocket?"

Hawke blinked in surprise and blurted, "Nothing."

"Then you shouldn't mind if I take a look,"
Donovan said. "Hand it over."

"No."

Seaman Burroughs jammed his M16 into the base
of the officer's spine. "Do as the captain says, sir."

Reluctantly, General Hawke slowly unbuttoned
the flap on the pocket and started to draw out a
red notebook. Abruptly, with a flick of his arm, he
hurled it at the water.

Donovan saw the notebook land with a light
splash two feet out. He sprang to the river's edge and
quickly waded in up to his ankles before the notebook could sink or become waterlogged. Scooping it

.e walked from the Potomac, his shoes, socks, and part of his pants soaked.

"Damn you all to hell," General Hawke growled.

Mystified, Donovan flipped the spiral notebook open. The contents were handwritten, and the first few pages contained names and three-digit telephone numbers, presumably extensions at Raven Rock. The next several pages were of more interest. They contained the names of facilities such as Mount Weather and other bunkers along with nine-digit codes. He didn't know what to make of them. Then he came to the last page and hit the jackpot. Under the heading of "Secured Armories" were the names of a dozen locations scattered throughout the country, some on the East and West coasts. He realized the sites must be where secret government stockpiles of weapons had been stored and the germ of an idea took root in his brain. "Thank you, General," he said, pocketing the notebook. "This will come in handy."

"You won't live long enough to make any use of it," Hawke stated angrily.

"We'll see."

The transfer operation was going smoothly. Ten inflatables were now involved in taking survivors to the sub. By packing five into each craft, the crewmen were rapidly completing their task.

But it wasn't going fast enough to suit Donovan. He surveyed the horizon on all sides, knowing there must be Dragonflies out there somewhere awaiting the signal to attack. The corps wasn't about to let *Liberator* escape. He impatiently urged his men on, and when the last of the prisoners was being rowed toward the ship he looked at President Murphy. "What happens next is up to you. I'd rather leave in peace, but if you start something, rest assured we'll finish it."

"Brave words for a man whose days are numbered."

An inflatable was waiting, Percy and C̶r̶o̶w̶ already in it.

"Get in," Donovan commanded Burroughs, and covered the three hostages with the Colt as he backed toward the water. "Stand right where you are and keep those five choppers on the ground until we're gone. Our Walther will cut you to ribbons if you make a move."

None of the trio spoke.

Donovan climbed into the inflatable and sat down. The two crewmen began paddling furiously. He stared at the president, torn by conflicting emotions, wishing things had been different but knowing the die was cast. There could be no turning back. Neither Murphy nor the two corps officers so much as moved an arm as the inflatable covered the seventy yards to *Liberator*.

With a sense of supreme relief Donovan stepped onto the starboard diving plane. Several of the crewmen offered warm greetings. He acknowledged them, handed over the transceiver and the Franchi, and ordered the inflatables to be stowed below immediately. Percy took charge of the last bunch of survivors, urging them down the forward hatch.

Donovan hastened up the ladder to the topside bridge. The moment he cleared the rail Alex was there, rushing into his arms and hugging him close, heedless of the looks of the watch officer and two seamen manning the bridge. He embraced her pliant form, inhaling the sweet scent of her hair and skin, and almost planted a passionate kiss on her lips. Instead, he regained his self-control and pulled back. "I take it you missed me?"

"Not at all," Alex said, her moist eyes betraying her true feelings. Then she gave him a playful punch on the arm. "Just don't make a habit of leaving me behind."

"You'd best get below," Donovan told her.

192

ut—" Alex began, studying his face. She abruptly nodded and made for the hatch.

Donovan moved to the aft rail. He stared over the side of the tower to find Flazy supervising the Walther crew. Smith glanced up and Donovan waved and shouted, "Be ready to fire on my command."

"Sure thing. And welcome back, Skipper."

Wasting no time, Donovan next stepped to the intercom. "Communications?"

"Jennings here, sir."

"Any sign of an attack?"

"Not yet."

"Patch me through to the helm."

A second later Helmsman Hooper came on. "Hooper here, Captain."

"Get us the hell out of here. Stick to the outbound shipping channel. Speed, thirty knots. Watch out for obstructions and be ready to dive at a moment's notice."

"Aye, Captain," Hooper responded.

Donovan glanced at the warrant officer and the pair of crewmen. "Down you go, gentlemen. Report to your battle stations."

The trio promptly obeyed.

Wondering if there was anything he'd missed, Donovan peered over the rail at the crewmen scurrying to get the inflatables below. Percy was goading them on. For once there was no sign of Gloria Harrison.

*Liberator* began to swing about, her streamlined bow cleaving the surface smoothly. On the beach the president, the general, and Captain Rockwood were still rooted in place. The five black helicopters rested quietly. All appeared serene.

Suddenly the intercom blared to life.

"Captain, multiple airborne targets ten miles to the northwest and closing fast. Speed, one hundred and eighty miles an hour. Dragonflies, sir."

193

"As soon as they're within range and we h₂ laser lock, open fire."

"Yes, sir," Jennings said, then added excitedly. "More targets have just appeared, sir. Three choppers are closing in from the south. Range, nine miles. Speed, one hundred and sixty miles an hour."

Donovan swept the southern horizon. Those three Dragonflies must be the same ones previously assigned to patrol the Potomac in *Liberator*'s vicinity. Major General Rainey, or whoever was now in command, must have sent them south and was now employing his aerial forces in a classic pincer movement. He glanced at Blakistone Island and saw the rotors on all five Dragonflies spinning at top speed. With a start he realized they were about to lift off and undoubtedly open fire.

President Murphy, General Hawke, and Captain Rockwood were sprinting toward the middle copter.

In four bounds Donovan reached the aft rail. "Flazy!" he bellowed. "Don't let those choppers get into the air."

The Walther PB AutoStrafe opened up seconds later, shattering the still air with its chattering cadence of destruction. At such short range the effects were devastating. Starting from right to left as the machine gun crew worked the AutoStrafe in a tight arc, the Dragonflies on shore were riddled with high-velocity armor-piercing ammo.

Rounds punctured the cockpit of the first Dragonfly, causing sparks and smoke to pour out. The second chopper tried to rise when flames shot out from under the rotor and it fell straight down. All three of the remaining Dragonflies managed to become airborne, flitting dozens of feet into the air in the blink of an eye. The AutoStrafe crew compensated, tracking the whirlybirds upward, firing all the time, pouring hundreds of rounds into the three craft. Struck in its power plant, the middle gonfly abruptly plummeted, spewing gray-and-black smoke.

Donovan stood riveted to the tableau, keenly aware that if the machine gun crew failed, *Liberator* would be sent to the bottom.

Murphy, Hawke, and Rockwood had flattened when the AutoStrafe cut loose and were now hugging the ground.

The fourth Dragonfly pilot foolishly tried to turn and flee, swinging his aircraft broadside. Instantly it was raked from nose to tail, dotted with dozens of holes. Then, unexpectedly, the copter exploded.

A fireball blossomed, billowing outward and enveloping the last Dragonfly in a ball of red-and-orange flame at the selfsame second the last pilot fired a rocket from the aircraft's port rocket launcher. The blast bucked the Dragonfly upward as the rocket streaked forward.

Donovan, watching the rocket speed toward the submarine, felt his blood transform to ice. He gripped the rail hard, bracing for the inevitable impact, but to his astonishment the rocket zipped by a dozen yards overhead. The trajectory was off! The explosion had buffeted the Dragonfly sufficiently to ruin the firing angle. He pivoted in time to view the rocket smack into the Potomac River hundred of yards off, blowing a tremendous geyser of water skyward.

The machine gun crew was cheering.

Elation brought a smile to Donovan's lips, a short-lived smile as he realized they were far from in the clear. He cupped his hands to his mouth and shouted to Chief Smith and the gunnery detail, "Well done. Now get the Walther below, pronto."

Without waiting for their reaction, Donovan moved to check on the men handling the inflatables. He peered down just in time to see the forward hatch being closed. All of the inflatables and crewmen were now safely below, with one notable exception.

Executive Officer Percy was climbing the la... within ten feet of the top. He saw Donovan and grinned. "First blood to our side."

"The battle isn't over yet," Donovan said grimly, and gave his friend a hand clambering onto the topside bridge.

*Liberator* was just completing her hundred-and-eighty-degree turn. She picked up speed rapidly, climbing to thirty knots, white spray shooting off her bow and sides.

"Any incoming?" Percy said, grabbing the splash rail for support.

Donovan nodded. He looked over his shoulder and saw three familiar figures standing at the water's edge. President Murphy was vigorously shaking his right fist in the air and shouting, his words indistinct because of the distance. The message, however, came through loud and clear. Donovan knew he had an enemy for life.

"All we have to do is reach the Atlantic," Percy commented. "They can't touch us once we're cruising at a depth of five hundred feet."

Turning, Donovan anxiously surveyed the air space to their north. It was twenty-five miles to the ocean and Dragonflies would be hounding them every foot of the way. How the hell could they hope to survive running a nonstop gauntlet of missiles and rockets?

As if in confirmation of his thoughts, the intercom crackled to life and Communications Officer Jennings exclaimed, "Captain! Cruise missile coming in, five miles astern!"

## 22

Astern? Donovan spun, gazing out over the rudder along the expanse of the Potomac River to their rear. The very thought of a cruise missile streaking to intercept *Liberator* caused his skin to break out in goose bumps. He stabbed the intercom. "Five miles? Why didn't we pick it up sooner?"

"Radar barely detected the damn thing as it was," Jennings responded. "It's coming straight down the middle of the Potomac, almost skimming the surface."

Donovan knew how versatile a cruise missile could be. Once launched, it was guided by a tiny onboard computer until within radar range of its target, at which point the radar seeker component automatically engaged and the missile would lock onto the target and close in for the kill.

"Sixty seconds to impact," Jennings reported. "I've initiated jamming."

"Tell Weapons Control to try and get a laser lock, just in case," Donovan commanded, knowing the chances of the laser scoring a hit on an object moving at over six hundred miles an hour were slim to nonexistent. They must rely on *Liberator*'s sophisticated jamming equipment, which was at that moment engaged in an electronic battle of wits with the incoming cruise missile's radar seeker.

"Weapons Control informed," Jennings said.

197

"Forty-five seconds until impact."

Both Donovan and Percy stared back along the Potomac, their faces reflecting their controlled apprehension.

"Where did the sons of bitches launch it from?" Percy wondered aloud.

"Your guess is as good as mine," Donovan replied, and buzzed Jennings again. "What about those Dragonflies?"

"Both the six to the north and the three to the south have just slowed and changed direction. They appear to be making for a point a few miles ahead of us, Skipper."

Of course they were, Donovan reflected. If the cruise missile failed to destroy *Liberator,* then the corps would be waiting downriver, probably at a narrow point where the sub wouldn't be able to maneuver freely, blocking the escape route. The choppers would probably fan out over the water and blast *Liberator* the moment the ship came within range.

"Thirty seconds until impact," Jennings said. "Missile has not deviated from its course."

Donovan came to a quick decision. He couldn't rely on just the jamming when the lives of everyone on board might be extinguished in half a minute. Sometimes a missile could be fooled by other than electronic means. Bright light or sources of extreme heat could confuse a sensitive radar seeker and cause a missile to fix on a false target. He knew of an incident during the Central American War where a quick-thinking officer on a destroyer decoyed an incoming missile by shooting up flares; the missile arced up after a bursting flare and narrowly missed the destroyer. "Open fire with the laser," he order crisply. "Random firing into the air off the stern."

Three seconds later Weapons Control swung into action and the twin turrets began sending shafts of

..sh green light into the atmosphere.

Percy had his eyes glued to the Potomac. "I admire a man who never says die," he quipped, "even if your brainstorm has a snowball's chance in hell of working."

Donovan said nothing. He waited for the cruise missile to appear. The crackling roar of its propulsion unit heralded its arrival and he saw the gleaming nose materialize as a bright pinpoint and grow rapidly larger. It was flying at a height of only three or four feet above the water, a glistening metallic harbinger of destruction about to cause *Liberator*'s premature demise.

"Oh, God," Percy breathed.

They saw the missile speeding unerringly toward them. The range narrowed in a heartbeat to hundreds of yards. Then, when impact seemed a certainty, either *Liberator*'s jamming or the laser flashes had the desired effect; the missile abruptly banked steeply upward and sailed directly over the sub in a graceful but noisy arc, missing the topside bridge by a mere dozen yards. It kept going until lost to sight somewhere down the river.

Donovan realized he was gripping the splash rail so hard his fingers were hurting. He let go and grinned, his finger pressing the transmit button. "Mr. Jennings, cease fire."

"Cease fire it is, sir."

The turrets quit discharging beams.

"Where there's one there might be more," Percy mentioned, scouring the landscape right and left.

"I know," Donovan agreed. He stepped over to the side and watched Flazy and the gun crew take the machine gun below, the whole time racking his brain for a way out of their dilemma. What with being hemmed in by the relatively shallow and narrow confines of the waterway and facing adversaries whose maneuverability and lightning speed made them near impossible targets to hit,

*Liberator* was at a tactical disadvantage. But ⹀⹀ must be something he could do to even the odds.

He saw the hatch close and hastened to Percy. "Down we go. You first."

The executive officer obeyed with alacrity.

Donovan paused for a last glimpse around, then quickly went below, securing the hatch behind him. Percy was waiting, and together they hurried to the bridge, where every crew member was intently hunched over a monitor or console, acutely aware their lives depended on their performance.

Alex stood by the swivel chair.

"Dive, Mr. Hooper," Donovan directed as he took his seat and stared at the holographic display shimmering in front of the helmsman's post. There were the tiny icons representing the Dragonflies, converging a few miles ahead. "Take us down to periscope depth."

"Yes, sir," Hooper said.

Leaning over, Alex gently placed her hand on top of his, a fleeting contact with a world of meaning. "Was that as close as I think it was?"

"Closer."

*Liberator* began to gracefully sink below the foaming surface, compressed air hissing from the open vents of her ballast tanks as water flooded in at the bottom. The process of flooding the tanks took time, precious minutes in which *Liberator* was especially vulnerable.

Donovan concentrated on the icons. Thankfully, none were heading toward the ship. As he'd predicted, the Dragonflies had taken up positions in a line stretching completely across the river. "Report, Mr. Jennings."

"Targets are stationary, sir. Range, four miles. Radar is not picking up anything else. We're monitoring—" Jennings broke off in mid-sentence and twisted a dial. "Correction, Captain. Two more Dragonflies to the northwest. Range, ten miles."

paused. "But they're not heading our way."

"Where, then?"

"To Blakistone Island."

Donovan drummed his fingers on the chair arm. Those choppers would undoubtedly pick up the president and take him back to Raven Rock.

"We've been monitoring conversations between the pilots in the Dragonflies up ahead," Jennings said. "Commands and acknowledgments, mostly. They're very professional."

"Tell me about it," Donovan said dryly. He debated whether to try to run the gauntlet at flank speed and discarded the idea as certain suicide. The nine Dragonflies would unleash a hail of rockets and missiles that would reduce *Liberator* to charred wreckage. But it wouldn't do any good to stop and wait for the 'copters to come toward the sub. They'd still be in the same boat.

The inadvertent pun made him grin, which must have seemed terribly out of place given the circumstances and the palpable air of tension gripping the bridge crew, because Alex leaned forward and gave him a quizzical look. "Just thinking," he said, and studied the holograph, noting the depth under the keel and the configuration of the shoreline. If only there was somewhere they could hide.

Then it hit him.

The obvious solution.

He gripped the chair arm, his mind racing. Think! he chided himself. What sort of submarine-detection devices were likely to be on those choppers? His best guess would be a variation on the Light Airborne Multi-Purpose System that had been the main anti-submarine warfare detector employed by U.S. military forces for some years now. Such systems relied on motion discrimination, sound detection, and electronic spectrum analysis to pinpoint the locations of submarines moving under the surface. The key word was *moving*. If a sub sat on the bottom,

making no sound, the LAMP system's effectiv ⌐
was severely impaired.

He recalled that the probe had revealed that those
helicopters sported a laser-scrambling system. Did
the system work as a defense against laser probes
only, or did it somehow inhibit an actual laser
attack? Not that it mattered in the long run. He
only had the one option. All he could do was keep
his fingers crossed and hope that the system worked
exclusively on probes.

"Mr. Hooper," Donovan declared, "all stop."

Heads were raised at the command.

"All stop, sir," the helmsman acknowledged.

Donovan waited until they were still in the water,
then glanced at Jennings. "Are the Dragonflies still
waiting for us?"

"Affirmative, Skipper."

"Good. Let them wait," Donovan said, facing front.
"What's the sounding?"

"Three hundred and twelve feet under the keel.
There's a lot of sediment, probably washed down from
upriver after the nuclear attack on Washington."

"Mr. Hooper, set us on the bottom."

"Yes, sir."

More heads swung toward the captain's chair.

Percy came over. He stared thoughtfully at the
dazzling display for a moment, then nodded and
smirked. "Are you thinking what I think you're
thinking?"

"Do you have a better idea?"

"No, sir," Percy said. "I think it's brilliant. The
water is murky and deep enough that they shouldn't
be able to spot us even from directly overhead."

"My thinking precisely."

No one else spoke as the huge sub slowly headed for the bottom of the Potomac. Such a maneuver was risky, even under the best of conditions.
The propellers could become fouled with muck or
even bent by buried boulders. Sometimes the bot-

. . . would buckle under the weight, wedging a submarine fast.

"Nice and easy, Mr. Hooper," Donovan advised.

Hooper's head bobbed a few times. His attention exclusively riveted to his monitors, especially the depth indicator, he was taking *Liberator* down at a snail's pace.

Cyclops accurately depicted the contours of the riverbed. *Liberator* angled toward a level area near the middle of the channel, settling as gently as a feather. A few dozen yards to the south lay the twisted remains of a huge ship, an inverted V on the screen, the shattered hulk broken nearly in half, the bow and the stern both buried.

"Any idea what that was?" Donovan asked.

"A tanker, Skipper," Jennings said. "Her sonar registry plate identifies her as the *Hawthorne*. She must have been on her way out to sea when the war broke out. There's no evidence of a spill or a slick, so she was probably empty."

Thank goodness, Donovan reflected. The world was polluted enough. Centuries would be required before some semblance of a normal, healthy environment was reestablished. "Mr. Hooper, sound off on our depth, please."

"One hundred feet to go, sir."

"Captain!" Jennings suddenly said. "Two of the Dragonflies are heading toward us. Speed, ninety miles an hour."

Donovan glanced at the display and saw the icons moving. What was this action? A reconnaissance patrol to ascertain *Liberator*'s position? "Get us down, Mr. Hooper."

"Seventy-five feet left, sir."

"The Dragonflies have increased speed to one hundred and fifty miles an hour," Jennings said.

"Sixty feet, Captain."

"One hundred and ninety miles an hour. Range three miles, Skipper."

"Fifty feet," Hooper said.

Jennings raised his voice. "Captain, sensors report detecting LAMPS emissions."

"All stop," Donovan barked. The choppers had activated their ASW detectors. At such a range it was unlikely the Dragonflies had picked up *Liberator* yet, but they just might if the sub continued to move. "Depth under the keel?"

"Thirty-seven feet," Hooper responded.

"That will have to do," Donovan said, frowning. He'd wanted to be lower. Three dozen feet wasn't much, though, and they might be close enough to the bottom so they wouldn't stand out like a sore thumb when the Dragonflies came closer. "Silent running," he ordered. "Inform Engineering I want the power plant cut back to the seven percent level."

Jennings nodded and relayed the instructions.

"What's the seven percent level?" Alex inquired.

"About as low as the reactor can go and still operate the electrical systems," Donovan explained. "It means the reactor will be running as quietly as possible."

"So the LAMPS can't pinpoint it?"

"Hopefully."

They watched the two icons grow larger as the Dragonflies narrowed the distance.

"Range, two miles," Jennings said.

Donovan mentally debated whether to launch a decoy. *Liberator* included in her arsenal torpedoes that carried sonar transducer units capable of mimicking the sounds of a submarine. The decoys broadcast typical engine and propeller noises, running off a miniature tape recorder, and could be used to fool an enemy into thinking the decoy was the real McCoy. He decided not to risk it. There was a chance the LAMPS operators might realize the ploy and trace the decoy's path back to its source.

"One mile," Jennings stated.

one hundred and ninety miles an hour the Dragonflies streaked overhead incredibly fast. Everyone on the bridge was riveted to the screen, each hoping the choppers would keep on going. The helicopter on the right did; the one on the left abruptly slowed, then stopped.

"Uh-oh," Percy said.

"What's wrong?" Alex asked, and perceived the answer the very next moment when in the blink of an eye the Dragonfly swooped back to hover directly over *Liberator*.

No one spoke. No one moved.

Donovan barely breathed, certain *Liberator* had been detected. Then he saw the Dragonfly begin to fly in a narrow circle and relaxed slightly.

"Has it found us?" Alex whispered.

Percy answered. "They don't know for sure we're here or they wouldn't be conducting a sweep. They must have picked up something, though, a trace of the reactor maybe."

The Dragonfly was flying in an ever-widening pattern.

Glancing at the remains of the tanker, Donovan realized that the proximity of so much steel would make ascertaining *Liberator*'s exact position extremely difficult. The LAMPS device would pick up an echo from the tanker which would overlap with the one from *Liberator* and give a false reading. Would it be sufficient to fool the LAMPS operator into thinking there was nothing but wreckage on the bottom?

The other Dragonfly returned and joined the first in conducting a search. They crisscrossed the Potomac a half-dozen times, each pass taking them farther from the sub. Finally they flew off toward Blakistone Island but only went half a mile before reversing direction and zipping off toward the formation waiting four miles downriver.

"Whew," Percy said after the two choppers flew by, breaking the strained silence that had prevailed since the Dragonflies conducted their sweep. "That was too close for comfort."

"What now?" Alex wondered.

"We wait," Donovan said.

"That's all?"

"With any luck those corps goons are confused right about now," Donovan elaborated. "They know we should be somewhere between Blakistone Island and them but they can't find us. They'll think we've somehow slipped through their net and they might just conduct a thorough search of the Potomac."

"Then they'll locate us for sure."

"Maybe not."

The two helicopters linked up with their companions.

"There's a lot of chatter taking place," Jennings reported. "They're discussing the situation and what to do about it."

"Come on," Donovan said. "Come to Papa."

A tense minute went by. Finally, strung out in a line, the nine helicopters advanced up the waterway.

"Mr. Jennings, tell Weapons Control I want a laser lock on each of those choppers," Donovan said.

"Yes, sir."

"You intend to take on all nine at once?" Alex asked skeptically.

"We'll initiate a computer-controlled firing sequence at just the right moment and keep our fingers crossed," Donovan replied. He watched the Dragonflies approach, his stomach in knots, wishing *Liberator* had been fitted with a few ship-to-air missiles instead of exclusively the ballistic nuclear variety. He thought of the list of armories he'd taken from General Hawke and had an inspiration. Perhaps, if *Liberator* survived, he'd stop at one of the sites on the way

207

back to Espiritu. There was one in Florida ~~~ wouldn't entail too great a detour. The delay would be worth it if he found armaments *Liberator* could use.

"The Dragonflies are two and a half miles off," Jennings said. "Speed is only forty miles an hour."

Donovan rested his elbow on the chair arm and propped his chin in his palm. The choppers were conducting an intense search-and-destroy effort, concentrating their combined LAMPS on a single stretch of river at a time. "Mr. Jennings, I want the lasers fired independently. The forward turret will start with the copters on the right, the aft turret with those on the left."

"Understood, Captain."

"How close will you let them get?" Alex asked.

"We'll fire when we can see the whites of their eyes," Donovan said.

The line of Dragonflies drew slowly nearer, maintaining a regularly spaced formation with perfect military precision.

"Explain something to me," Alex said.

"If I can."

"How is Cyclops able to indicate the precise position of those Dragonflies when we're too far down for you to use your radar?"

"Cyclops receives input data from a variety of sources, not just radar and sonar," Donovan said. "Anything we pick up—electronic emissions, radio broadcasts, sound waves, electromagnetic fluctuations—can be used by the computer to pinpoint a given object. Those babies are packed with electronic gear our sensors can detect even under water." He paused. "The range isn't as great as it would be if we were using radar, but usually we can pick up anything under five or six miles."

"If those guys were smart," Percy interjected, "they'd turn off their LAMPS and clam up until we showed ourselves."

Donovan straightened. He thought of how it had been back in the old days, when submerged subs were at the mercy of aerial adversaries since the sub operators had no way of knowing where their enemies were. Thanks to tremendous advances in subaqueous broadband receiver capability achieved shortly after the turn of the century, the Omega-class sub and a few others constructed immediately before the war were able to track aerial targets with astonishing precision.

"Range is down to half a mile," Jennings said.

Donovan let them come closer. If the Dragonflies were right on top of *Liberator* when he cut loose, the pilots wouldn't be able to react fast enough to evade the lasers. Or so he hoped.

"Seven hundred yards, sir."

The holographic display became the center of attention for practically everyone on the bridge. The Dragonflies flew steadily nearer and nearer.

Standing, Donovan took a step toward the display. This was it. The moment of truth. He listened to Jennings counting down the range.

"Five hundred yards."

Donovan was tempted to give the order but refrained. He didn't want to blow it now.

"Four hundred yards."

He looked at Alex, chiding himself for not leaving her on Espiritu where she would be safe. The prospect of her dying because of his selfishness sparked feelings of profound guilt. She noticed his look and gave him an encouraging smile, and at that moment he loved her more than he had ever loved anyone in his entire life.

"Two hundred yards."

Donovan took a breath and faced the screen. His fingernails bit into the palms of his hands. So many lives depended on his judgment. If he'd miscalculated, he shuddered to think of the consequences.

"One hundred yards," Jennings said. "Seven.. five yards."

Almost everyone was now staring at Donovan.

"Fifty yards."

*Not yet!* Donovan's mind shrieked.

"Twenty-five yards."

"Commence firing," Donovan commanded.

Both laser turrets opened up a fraction later, each blasting a bright beam of amplified light-frequency radiation at the Dragonflies, beams that could disrupt any electrical circuit, causing wires to fry and short-circuits to destroy components. Triggered by the computer, the lasers swept in from opposite ends of the line of choppers, firing at a rate no mere human reflexes could ever hope to match, searing each aircraft from nose to tail.

It was like a shooting gallery at a carnival, Donovan thought, watching the Dragonflies frantically veer off, some to the south, some to the north, their flight paths erratic, a few dipping drastically in altitude. Seconds later one hit the water. Another followed suit.

A cheer went up from the bridge crew.

"Cease firing. Mr. Hooper, take us up to periscope depth," Donovan said, sitting down.

A third Dragonfly went into a spiral and smashed into the Potomac.

None of the helicopters offered opposition as *Liberator* climbed from the murky depths of the river. Three reached the north shore and promptly landed. Two did the same to the south. The final chopper tried to flee to the northwest but went down well shy of land.

Donovan allowed himself the luxury of a broad grin. His strategy had worked marvelously. Now all that remained was to get the hell out of there before more Dragonflies showed up.

In no time *Liberator* levelled off much closer to the surface.

eriscope depth, sir," Hooper announced.

"Up scope and mast," Donovan directed, and moved over to the periscope for his first glimpse of the destruction he'd wrought. Smoke billowed from every Dragonfly. Those in the drink were rapidly sinking. Corps personnel in life jackets floated on the surface. So did several corpses.

"Captain," Jennings said, "radar has picked up six more Dragonflies. Bearing two-nine-zero. Range, eleven miles. Speed, one hundred and sixty. One of the choppers on the north shore is relaying a report to the incoming aircraft." He cocked his head as if listening to something in his headset. "And now we're being hailed, sir."

"We are?" Donovan repeated in surprise.

"President Murphy wants to speak to you."

Donovan reached the communications post in four bounds and took a proffered microphone from Jennings. "Pipe it through the speaker. I want everyone to hear."

"Here goes, sir," Jennings said, pressing buttons. The speaker blared to life with an irate voice.

" . . . to U.S.S. *Liberator*. Acknowledge, please. This is President Harry Murphy. Answer me, Donovan, damn you."

Donovan cleared his throat. "Donovan here, Murphy. What do you want?"

There was a short pause, then the incensed chief executive came on the line. "We're coming to get you, bastard! I know the trick you just pulled. It won't help you against us. I'm personally going to blow you out of the water."

Rage welled up in Donovan's breast, rage at the petty dictator who presumed to control the lives of everyone under him, the man who had transformed the land of the free and the home of the brave into a virtual concentration camp. Fate had played a cruel trick on the U. S. of A. Of all the possible successors to the presidential office, only Murphy

had survived, and only because the coward ha..
fled to Raven Rock at the onset of hostilities. If
not for—

Wait a minute.

An idea blossomed in Donovan's mind and he
smiled. If he was right about Murphy's character,
he had the key to escaping safely.

"Did you hear me?" Murphy snapped.

"Loud and clear," Donovan said. "But I'm afraid
you have your facts backwards."

"What do you mean?"

"I want you to call off the corps. Instruct your
Dragonflies to leave us alone or else."

Static crackled for five seconds before Murphy
took the bait. "Or else what?"

"Or else I launch a nuclear attack on Raven
Rock."

The bridge crew exchanged glances. Percy snickered and slapped his thigh. Alex arched her brows
but said nothing.

Murphy's response was almost a whisper. "You
wouldn't dare!"

"What have I got to lose?" Donovan retorted.
"You've given me no choice. If I'm going down, I'm
taking Raven Rock with me."

"You saw Site R. There's no way a nuclear warhead could damage that bunker."

"You're right," Donovan said. "A single nuclear
warhead couldn't. But what about twenty? If you
don't call off your dogs, I swear I'll launch every
Mark 97N on board at your precious complex and
vaporize the whole damn place." He lowered the
mike and stared at the speaker, his nerves tingling.
Everything depended on Murphy's decision. Would
the man let his insane thirst for power get the
better of him? Would Murphy sacrifice all for the
sake of vengeance?

The hiss of static filled the bridge for half a minute.

ı believe you would, you son of a bitch," the chief executive growled at last. A sigh fluttered over the airwaves. "All right, Donovan. You win this round. But don't think this is the end of it. You're a traitor, mister, and sooner or later you'll get yours."

Donovan handed the microphone back and turned. He saw the relief on every face, the admiration in many eyes.

"The six Dragonflies are veering off," Jennings reported.

Spontaneous whoops of joy greeted the disclosure. Men patted each other on the back and beamed happily.

Alex came across the bridge in a rush, heedless of the crew, and flew into Donovan's arms. He embraced her, feeling the tension drain from his body, elated at the outcome. Now she would live. Now they would have a chance to rear their child, to know the joy of being a family.

Now they had a future.

It was that night, as *Liberator* cruised southward along the Eastern Seaboard toward Florida, that Jennings received the shortwave transmission from the powerful transmitter the colonists had installed on Espiritu. He promptly notified the captain, who was in his quarters with Alex.

Donovan hastened to the bridge and heard his brother's voice issuing from the speaker. Percy, with Gloria Harrison at his side, was talking to Charlie. The executive officer promptly gave Donovan the mike.

"Hey, little brother. I take it the island is still in one piece."

"Very funny, Tom. If you ever acquire a sense of humor you'll be a load of laughs."

Grinning, Donovan leaned on the console and asked, "Seriously, how are things going? Have you taken care of the dogs?"

213

"Boy, have we," Charlie replied.

"Did you kill them?"

"Uhhh, not quite," Charlie said. As he spoke a peculiar yipping arose in the background, almost drowning out his voice.

"What was that noise?"

"Just Fido."

Donovan wasn't sure if he'd heard correctly. "Fido?"

"A puppy. You see, that's the reason I've contacted you, big brother. We don't have a lot of canned food we can spare, and trying to catch enough game to feed thirty-one dogs is a real pain in the butt."

"Thirty-one dogs?"

"Yeah," Charlie said. "So on behalf of all the colonists, I'd like to ask a favor."

"Thirty-one dogs?"

"Isn't that what I said? Now what about that favor?"

"What kind of favor?"

"Would you bring back some dog food?"

They survived Armageddon
to sail the oceans
of a ravaged nightmare world

**OMEGA SUB**           76049-5/$2.95 US/$3.50 Can
On top secret maneuvers beneath the polar ice cap, the
awesome nuclear submarine U.S.S. *Liberator* surfaces to
find the Earth in flames. Civilization is no more—great
cities have been reduced to smoky piles of radioactive ash.

**OMEGA SUB #2: COMMAND DECISION**
          76206-4/$2.95 US/$3.50 Can

**OMEGA SUB #3: CITY OF FEAR**
          76050-9/$2.95 US/$3.50 Can

**OMEGA SUB #4: BLOOD TIDE**
          76321-4/$3.50 US/$4.25 Can

**OMEGA SUB #5: DEATH DIVE**
          76492-X/$3.50 US/$4.25 Can

**OMEGA SUB #6: RAVEN RISING**
          76493-8/$3.50 US/$4.25 Can

# JAMES ELLROY

# POLICE THRILLERS by
# "THE ACKNOWLEDGED MASTER"
## *Newsweek*

# ED McBAIN

| | |
|---|---|
| CALYPSO | 70591-5/$4.50 US/$5.50 Can |
| DOLL | 70082-4/$4.50 US/$5.50 Can |
| HE WHO HESITATES | 70084-0/$4.50 US/$5.50 Can |
| ICE | 67108-5/$4.99 US/$5.99 Can |
| KILLER'S CHOICE | 70083-2/$4.50 US/$5.50 Can |
| BREAD | 70368-8/$4.50 US/$5.50 Can |
| 80 MILLION EYES | 70367-X/$4.50 US/$5.50 Can |
| HAIL TO THE CHIEF | 70370-X/$4.50 US/$5.50 Can |
| LONG TIME NO SEE | 70369-6/$4.50 US/$5.50 Can |

## Don't Miss These Other Exciting Novels

| | |
|---|---|
| WHERE THERE'S SMOKE | 70372-6/$3.50 US/$4.50 Can |
| GUNS | 70373-4/$3.99 US/$4.99 Can |
| GANGS! | 70757-8/$3.50 US/$4.25 Can |
| VANISHING LADIES | 71121-4/$4.50 US/$5.50 Can |
| BIG MAN | 71123-0/$4.50 US/$5.50 Can |
| DEATH OF A NURSE | 71125-7/$4.50 US/$5.50 Can |